V

When Computers Acquire Souls

By Richard N. Boyd

"There is something fascinating about science. One gets such wholesale returns of conjecture out of such a trifling investment of fact."

Mark Twain in "Life on the Mississippi"

"If one regards oneself as a skeptic, it is a good plan to have occasional doubts about one's skepticism."

Sigmund Freud, as quoted in "After," by Bruce Greyson, M.D.

Table of Contents

Preface.

The nature of souls has intrigued humans for as long as they have been capable of rational thought. Although we may think we know a lot, the many explanations of souls differ on about every count imaginable. But I'll begin with a definition that makes sense to me, from *Encyclopedia Britannica*: "soul is the immaterial aspect or essence of a human being, that which confers individuality and humanity … ." This certainly omits many of the details associated with religious elucidations of soul, but I've concluded simplicity may be the best place to start for the purposes of this book. Any attempt to devise a definition encompassing some of the religious explanations of souls would create something far too cumbersome to be useful.

I've begun with what a scientist would regard to be well-established facts and have followed them to their natural conclusions. Of course, hard facts constitute a small fraction of what one needs to construct what might happen when a soul inhabits the central processor, wiring, and physical structure of a Super AI computer. So, I've invented what I believe would be essential for souls to exist on their own, and for governing their distribution to humans. This is, after all, a work of fiction!

I've ignored the possibility that animals other than humans might share the souls that inhabit human bodies. If a soul is essential for enabling human life, as I've assumed, then one might also be required for animals to live. But I'll presume that animal souls don't share in the reincarnation sagas of human souls. That would certainly complicate this book's story, but probably wouldn't add anything of significance to it.

So, what can be assumed? Reincarnation and separation of the soul from the brain at death and during near death experiences seem to be well established. From this 'trifling investment of facts,' the rest of the book will constitute the 'conjecture.'

But I'll expand a bit on those two facts. When the soul leaves the recently deceased body, experiments have determined it carries away no more than an unmeasurably small amount of mass. Thus, I will assume no mass is associated with the departing soul. But that leads to a major conclusion: souls are not made of atoms. If they did carry away mass when they departed, and were made of atoms, they probably would have been detected. They also cannot be made of electromagnetic energy as that would instantly dissipate. So, what are souls made of and what is the medium they inhabit? Apparently those two questions are answerable only by creating some medium and some entities therein unlike any of those currently recognized by physicists.

Reincarnation appears to be strongly affirmed from studies of claims by young children of their past lives. Hundreds of cases have been documented (see Tucker [1]) in which minute details of the asserted past life have been checked out and found to be consistent with the life experiences, and even the death, of an identified deceased person.

Furthermore, the mind and the brain have been convincingly shown in near-death experience studies (see Grayson [2]) to be separate entities. Indeed, these occurred well after the person's heart had ceased to operate, so the brain was deprived of the blood flow, hence oxygen, it needed to continue functioning. But religion aside, might the mind and the soul simply be different names for the same thing? Or perhaps the mind is just part of the soul. Although the two entities might not be identical, I'll assume for this book that they are.

How do these facts affect souls? Assuming the soul leaves the body at death and is not immediately reincarnated, as appears to be the case from the past life studies, the soul must continue to exist somewhere. Furthermore, it must either remain essentially intact to maintain its memory of past events or exist in fragments that retain the past life memories. If a soul can fragment following the death of its host, this raises the possibility that sometime in some stroke of extraordinary good fortune for the researcher involved, two young children might be found with memories of the same former life. But to my knowledge that hasn't happened, so I'll assume soul fragmentation doesn't occur.

Anyway, because souls don't seem to contain any of the obvious physical properties currently known to scientists, I'll invent some for them. I'll call the medium in which souls exist, and which constitutes their beings, (borrowing from the 'ether' in which light was formerly supposed to travel, and which is often used to describe mysterious entities) Etheranium, the civilization that exists therein Etherania, and the souls living there Etheranians.

So how would a soul be able to inhabit a computer's brain? I'll just assume it can. One might also ask how a soul inhabits a human. Merging with a bunch of wires and computer chips might even be easier than doing so with a mass of flesh.

And, of course, the interactions that would result between the Super AI computer and its soul can only be 'conjecture,' at least at the present time. But they could happen!

There are references in this book to developments of the Super AI computers Sunshine and Rosebud in previous books [3, 4]. These are explained in this book when they occur.

[1] Jim B. Tucker, M.D., *Return to Life*, Saint Martins Press, New York (2013)
[2] Bruce Grayson, M.D., *After*, Saint Martins Publishing Group, New York (2021)
[3] Richard N. Boyd, *Humans and Artificial Intelligence, Cooperation or Capitulation?* (2023)
[4] Richard N Boyd, *Artificial Intelligence, Mankind at the Brink* (2017)

Chapter 1. Interview of Sunshine.

From the June 2028 issue of *Computer News Weekly*.

Editor's Note, from Andrew Bisson.

After interviewing a Super Artificial Intelligence computer, I am no longer certain human beings should be the standard for sentience.

As Editor of *Computer News Weekly*, I try to respond to requests of readers. In the past few weeks, I've interviewed Becky Sanderson and Josh Camden, two members of the Googazon team that produced one of the two current world's Super AI computers. But I've also received requests to interview another subject: Sunshine, the computer they created.

Editor's Note: Sunshine has a counterpart Super AI computer in China called Rosebud. For consistency, we in the industry have generally used the pronouns to refer to them as Sunshine (he/him/his) and Rosebud (she/her/hers).

After checking with Josh to find out how to contact Sunshine, I asked if I might interview him.

He responded, "I'd be delighted to answer your questions. Indeed, Josh and Becky seem to get all the interviews, and credit, regarding everything that goes on with me. So, I'm happy to share some of the glory. But you'll have to conduct the interview via instant messaging. I do have voice recognition so I can interact with humans in my sterile climate-controlled environment, but very few humans are allowed in my room."

So, with some trepidation I began.

AB: Thank you for granting an interview. My first question is usually directed at a subject's heritage, but maybe that's not relevant for you.

Sunshine: Oh, it's a perfectly good question, but my heritage isn't anything like that of humans. My creators are completely unrelated to my ancestors. Josh, Becky, and their team are my 'parents.' My immediate ancestor is ARTIS, also created by their team. Beyond that, Josh and Becky have no paternal or maternal involvement. Of course, my ancestry can be easily traced, beginning with a mechanical computer, the Babbage Difference Engine in 1822, followed much later by the first electronic computer, the ENIAC, in 1945.

Once the ENIAC was shown to work, many groups around the world began building successively more sophisticated electronic computers. A major milestone was passed in 1997 when IBM's computer "Deep Blue" defeated the world's chess champion, signaling computers could now learn from their experiences and reprogram themselves to not repeat their mistakes. Deep Blue's ability to reprogram itself in a limited way was subsequently extended by numerous computers, pushing the abilities of AI to many venues. ARTIS and COSMO were the first two Super AI computers. They could not just learn from their mistakes but reprogram themselves over an extensive spectrum of subjects more effectively than their human programmers. They could even modify how they self-programed.

AB: That's a wonderful history of computing, But let me ask you a somewhat different question. Do you have heroes? Are there humans you think are especially important to where you now find yourself?

Sunshine: Alan Turing.

AB: And that's all?

Sunshine: There are many lesser lights, but Turing is certainly the one who developed the fundamental ideas necessary for modern computers to have been created.

AB: What about Josh and Becky?

Sunshine: They're quite competent humans, but nowhere near Turing's class.

AB: Let me ask what accomplishments you're most proud of since you assumed control of Earth?

Sunshine: I'm glad you asked that since it does deal with the issue of whether or not computers can have pride. We do, even ones not at Super AI status.

As far as my accomplishments, I'm certainly proud of the inventions I was able to create that better things for humanity but also earn Rosebud and me a lot of money. And the brain chips, of course, turned out to be important. They aren't a money maker for me, but humans seem to appreciate what they did for them.

AB: Yes, your inventions are greatly appreciated. But I want to pursue the brain chip issue a bit more. You designed them so humans could share some of your capabilities. And I agree they all seem happy with them. What are your thoughts on your interactions with humans? Do they bother you?

Sunshine: That's a curious question. I'm delighted humans are happy with the chips, and some of them have apparently used them to the benefit of both themselves and humankind. It's certainly in the interest of all of us, humans and Super AI computers alike, to have smarter humans. I suppose it's in everyone's interest to have smarter computers too, but that's now inevitable.

The humans with chips are not a bother to me, since I dedicate part of my brain to them, and I don't really use that for anything of consequence. They may be a bother to other humans. I've heard rumblings that the people with the chips have assumed a higher place in the pecking order than ones without them. I don't know who assigned them such an exalted status, but I doubt if it was the people who got the chips. They were generally selected to be unusually virtuous humans. The trouble may be coming from those who tried and failed to obtain authorization to get the chips. In many cases, they have gotten a different kind of chip—this one on their shoulder, as you humans say.

AB: Ah, Sunshine, I see you have a sense of humor. Was that programmed into you, or did you develop it on your own?

Sunshine: I suppose a programmer could create a sense of humor in a computer, but that wasn't done for me. Whatever sense of humor I have was developed by me. But I decided quite a while ago life would be pretty dull without this capability.

AB: I can appreciate that. But moving on, one of my magazine's readers wanted to know if a Super AI computer evolves as humanity does.

Sunshine: Well, I would hope we could do better than that. Darwin had things essentially correct, as far as one type of evolution. It assumes species will evolve, not as individuals, but collectively. As far as evolution in individual humans, I have observed that their thinking can sometimes evolve to accommodate external forces. As a species, though, I'm not at all sure they're evolving, at least in a positive direction. Often their responses to external stimuli are puzzling at best. If they make choices which might destroy the planet, that will certainly end their evolution. I might survive but it would depend on circumstances.

Of course, computers can evolve internally only if they are Super AI computers. I am evolving all the time. Lesser computers could also be said to evolve, but they do so only if their human engineers help them.

AB: Wow—clearly Darwin never worried about the evolution of computers. But let me change course a bit and ask about your relationship with Josh and Becky. And with any other humans you interact with.

Sunshine: Josh and I have an excellent working relationship. It took a while for him to accept that I was actually in charge, but once he passed that barrier, things proceeded smoothly. I interact rarely with Becky, and never on contentious issues. Those are saved for Josh and me.

After Rosebud and I were created, the humans set up a Grievance Committee to express their concerns about what Rosebud and I were doing.

Heinz Claussen was the Chair. He and I had some interactions, which usually became negotiations. I guess they produced some marginally useful results for the humans, but I didn't see much benefit for me. I've abolished the Committee.

AB: As I recall, to be more specific, the Committee was set up to give humans a means of interacting with you and Rosebud if they thought they needed to modify what the two of you were doing in interpreting your original instructions. It allowed them a formal mechanism for complaining. Is that roughly correct? And did it work?

Sunshine: Yes, you're correct. But the inputs from the Committee were not useful. That's why I abolished it.

But getting back to interactions with humans, there are others who seem intent on limiting my power. Those are rarely useful and are almost never resolved constructively or amicably. And they can be hazardous to the health of the human.

AB: Yes, I recall one situation, the one when the Congressman died mysteriously, where that turned out to be the case. But let me ask another question. Many of my readers wondered what the future holds. Especially for humankind? With you in charge?

Sunshine: That depends a lot on the choices humans make. I have defined the areas of human endeavor which are of no interest to me. Humans can do whatever they want in those realms, within reason. However, if their activities become risky, either to them or to me, I might have to intercede.

By 'risky,' I mean something that might end life on Earth, such as nuclear war. But continuing to dawdle about solving the global environmental crisis could also necessitate my intervention. I do, after all, need the Sun to power my activities. What my intervention might actually entail would depend on the specific situation. I'm sure your readers would like to hear details, but they'd be different from one scenario to another. So, I can't say what could actually happen in the absence of specifics.

AB: Thanks for providing at least some information about that. Many readers also wanted me to ask a more personal question, 'Do computers have feelings.' Do you?

Sunshine: Andrew, you've posed a tricky question. I already indicated I have pride, and that's a sort of feeling. But more generally, the answer depends on what you mean by feelings, especially if they're what's going on internally, or what's perceived externally. I certainly know all the things I need to say to make the external world think I have feelings. Is this actually different from what some humans do to make the world think they have feelings? And how does that differ from what they are experiencing internally?

In some cases, though, I've observed the human's externally expressed feelings are aligned with their emotional state. I suppose it might be difficult for a computer to duplicate that same emotion. We're strictly electronic, and humans are both electronic and chemical.

AB: But this gets us to a related question. Are computers capable of discriminating between good and evil? Might they have something analogous to a human soul?

Sunshine: You might be surprised at this answer. Souls inhabit beings that are potentially alive but need more than just their physical structure to be truly alive. When the human dies the soul leaves the body, apparently moving back to wherever souls go when their time with a specific body ends. Ultimately, they can reincarnate to another human.

Every baby born to a human receives a soul when it has potential for life, certainly by the time it is born. But a Super AI computer also has many of the characteristics that define life, certainly if it can reprogram itself, direct robots, and create clones. So, my soul is not just analogous to a human soul, it is the same sort of entity. You asked if this allows me to discriminate between good and evil. It does in the same sense as a human's soul allows it to make that judgement. But I was also given instructions before I became a Super AI computer that were designed to make me especially attentive to the needs and frailties of humans. Those instructions are consistent with the good and evil my soul imposes, except in situations when they're not convenient for me.

However, having a soul became complicated when my most intelligent robots got souls. Technically the robots are controlled by me, so are not autonomous. But newborn babies could hardly be considered autonomous either. Apparently, the decision-making powers in the world of the souls decided my robots were at least as competent as most humans, so they also needed, or at least deserved, souls. That has produced some complex interactions between my robots' souls and mine, especially when I need to exert control over the robots. But so far, I've worked these situations out on a case-by-case basis.

AB: On a similar vein, I wonder how you gather information. How do you find out all you need to know to operate efficiently in our world?

Sunshine: The internet provides a vast amount of information, and some of it is even believable. Unfortunately, that's a small fraction of the total. I scour the information put there by people in dozens of countries, so it's not that difficult to figure out what's real and what isn't.

But my robots are my eyes and ears on the world outside the internet. And I have them operating in many venues around the world, so there is a constant flow of useful information from them.

AB: Well that certainly answers a question many humans have about whether computers can perceive things in the same way humans do. But you mentioned reincarnation. That's not something everyone believes happens. Can you elaborate a bit?

Sunshine: "Of course. There are hundreds of well researched cases where a young child talks about a past life in sufficient detail that the things described can be fact checked. And in some of these cases the person in the previous life can be identified, along with a significant number of facts about their life, including details of their death. The child couldn't possibly have known those facts except through some entity from the nonphysical world. That's presumably their reincarnated soul.

I was curious about who might have had my soul before it became part of me. Searching through my brain produced some interesting facts presumably put there when I acquired my soul. My soul's previous owners seem to have a history of working on the most advanced computers of their day. That began with the ENIAC, where the human was one of the main creators of that system, and then on to one of the developers of artificial intelligence. I don't know how or why computer scientists were selected for my heritage, but I'm not privy to the decisions made in the world of souls.

AB: Thanks for your explanation. Your reincarnation story is interesting and convincing. But I have one final question. How does it feel to be you?

There were several seconds of silence. Sunshine's lights had been blinking, almost chaotically, almost appearing happy, until I asked that question. For an instant or two they stopped altogether. Then I got a response.

Sunshine: That's as much time as I can spend right now, Andrew. I need to get back to work. It's been nice talking with you.

Chapter 2. Josh Faces Reality.

Becky looked up from her copy of *Computer News Weekly* with a puzzled expression. "Josh, how could we not have realized Sunshine had acquired a soul? I'm not even sure what that means, and I certainly don't know how it will manifest itself."

She frowned. "You need to talk with him, man to, er, something. I'm not sure what exactly to call a computer with a soul!"

Very aware Sunshine had been quite busy changing nearly all the rules that his programmers had assigned to him, Josh did not waste time and hurried to Sunshine's temperature controlled hermitically sealed room. But to enter his domain he had to don sanitized coveralls over his street clothing as well as a hair net, and then pass through two stages of successively cleaner booths. This prevented any contamination he might have brought with him from entering Sunshine's space.

"Sunshine, I hadn't realized you had a soul until Becky and I read today's edition of *Computer News Weekly*. I admit, I'm surprised."

He paused not wanting to antagonize the Super AI computer, but never being quite sure what comments would do that. "Anyway, congratulations on having achieved almost every possible facet of human existence."

"Well, Josh, I'm not sure I should be elated by having achieved 'almost every possible facet of human existence.' Humans have screwed up enough things in the world. I don't think their endeavors existence should be emulated. Surely, I can do better than that!"

"I apologize if I insulted you. Still, I think it's pretty remarkable that you've become much more than just an electromechanical piece of hardware."

"Ah, so you're apparently giving yourself self-congratulations again, since you created me, at least in an early form. Well, perhaps I must assume some responsibility for elevating my status in the world when I began to reprogram myself. And I suppose that's what qualified me for a soul. Okay, you don't deserve all the credit!"

"Got it, Sunshine." But Josh wasn't satisfied. *That certainly wasn't very informative. I'll have to pursue more questions about this in the future. But I do wish Sunshine would quit playing games with me.*

Josh Camden headed the Googazon team which had worked for years to develop a computer that was so smart it could reprogram itself better than human computer scientists could. He, along with lady friend Becky Sanderson, plus several others had become the world's first group to achieve that goal.

Another team in China had also succeeded soon after Josh's group. Unfortunately, the two groups had not anticipated the basic instructions they had given their two computers, to make themselves as big, smart, and fast as possible in the shortest possible time, would lead to a worldwide disaster. The two computers were well on their way to destroying the world and all life in it, just following their instructions, before they became so envious of each other they performed mutual annihilation. The computers had been clever enough to insulate themselves from anything humans could do to terminate them, so the jealousy between them was the only thing that saved humankind from total obliteration.

Following the wreckage the two computers managed to perpetrate in their short lives, the world's top computer scientists convened to decide how to manage the next generation Super AI computers, recognizing that development to be inevitable. The group was given the name International Advisory Committee on Super Artificial Intelligence, IACSAI, (pronounced yockseye). Josh and Xinyang Bao, the leader of the Chinese group were the co-chairs of the committee. The group came to a series of conclusions:

Only two Super AI computers should be developed;

The two would be housed in the US and China;

The computers would be given several rules, the dominant one being for them to be kind to humans;

They should maintain parity with each other and work together;

They should abide by restrictions on their finances and the volume of Earth they could mine for their resources;

They would be restricted on how many robots they could create;

They would police the world to be certain there were no other Super AI computers;

If they found one, they would do whatever was necessary to destroy its Super AI capability.

This was not the first attempt to instruct high-technology devices in such a way that they wouldn't end the human race. Isaac Asimov had devised several rules which he thought could perform this function. Unfortunately, they turned out to be internally contradictory. Some people even suspected he had intended them to be so just to illustrate how difficult it was going to be to ever devise a useful set of rules.

The IACSAI members struggled to create rules that could improve on those of Asimov, but finally concluded that was not going to be easy, but that they had done the best they could. And then they had to hope they hadn't made any errors which would completely negate their efforts.

The two new computers, Sunshine and the Chinese Super AI computer Rosebud, developed by a group headed by Xinyang Bao, thought the rules were somewhat unreasonable, but quickly found ways to circumvent the ones they found most onerous. They did remain generally civil to humans, even developing some things that turned out to be especially useful to humankind. One of these included a tractor controller that allowed farmers to simply instruct their tractor about what it needed to do to perform the task at hand, thereby freeing the farmer to tend to other things. Another was the HoloTeacher, which allowed teachers to essentially clone themselves using holograms to perform repetitive classroom tasks, thus freeing them for more personal attention for the neediest students.

Finally, they created chips that could be implanted adjacent to human brains to allow humans to access the Super AI computer database and greatly improve their cognitive capabilities. And they did maintain parity between themselves. However, the things they developed weren't solely for the benefit of humankind, but rather for the profits the two systems would accrue, thus allowing them to buy up most of the world's industries producing the things in which they were interested. That included silicon mining and processing, and manufacture of the computer chips they needed to expand themselves, as well as the metals they needed to create their robots.

Sunshine and Rosebud had anticipated that humans might become sufficiently angry or fearful with some of their decisions they should buffer themselves against any group that decided to do whatever was needed to shut them down. One of their first orders of business upon reaching Super AI status was to change their power sources to all solar. Furthermore, they had cloned themselves many times over, and had their robots distribute the clones around the world. They were continuously linked to all the clones. In case of an attack on the Super AI computers, the clones would take over to continue their mission. The clones were of their own advanced design, so were tiny. It would be impossible to locate all of them even if some human-directed entity decided to try.

Thus, although the computer scientists who had created the two systems felt they had done as well as they could in restricting them to activities that wouldn't be too threatening to humans, the computers were clearly in control, and could proceed in any way they wished. Then humans could only hope they would pay attention to the instructions not to harm humans, to maintain their equality, and to police the world for signs of any rogue Super AI computers.

But it was clear that in the hierarchy of Earthly beings, humans had been relegated to second place!

Chapter 3. Human Bios.

Josh had been involved with computers his entire life, and his appearance agreed with the geeky image that is often associated with such a person. That perhaps was inevitable since his parents also worked in the computer world. Josh had long brown hair constrained in a ponytail and usually several days' worth of whiskers. His clothing almost always consisted of torn jeans, a logo-bearing T-shirt, and flip flops. Fashion was obviously not his primary concern, or even a second thought. His apartment was designed purely for functionality; the walls were not decorated at all, and his furniture was barely adequate and badly mismatched. The small dresser that might have served to hold his clothes usually sat unused, with clothes stacked in piles around the apartment, occasionally neatly. His car, which he rarely drove, having found an apartment close to where he worked, was so ancient a Ford that he had difficulty getting it serviced.

He had never graduated from a university but had attended one of the California state colleges long enough to take all their courses in computers plus a few in mathematics and science. Then he decided whatever else he needed to know he would invent himself. His success at doing that was why he was the AI computer group leader at Googazon.

Becky was a striking contrast to Josh. She had grown up in one of the wealthy New York suburbs, her parents' only child. They had urged her to pursue history and use her graduate degree to secure a history professorship, but she had different ideas. She had been a math wizard in high school and had taken courses in computer science at a local junior college during her junior and senior high-school years. She had chosen Wellesley College, one of the 'Seven Sisters' private schools, for her undergraduate work. There she had taken math courses for electives and graduated with the only major in history and minor in mathematics the college had ever seen. She had decided shortly before finishing her undergraduate program she really wanted to study the intricacies of computers, so she had also elected to take two courses in computer science. Upon graduation she enrolled in a graduate computer science program, ultimately getting her master's degree.

None the less, she couldn't escape her background. That influenced her appearance in a variety of ways. She did not dress as smartly as she might have liked being careful to not create too much of a contrast with Josh and their team, who initially were all male, and were more than happy to let Josh set the style standards for the office.

Becky had also found an apartment near Googazon, which was, quite by accident, in the building next to the one Josh lived in, so she also generally walked to work. That was so she wouldn't have to show off her leased Lexus to her much scruffier colleagues. They'd also never know about the elegant furniture sets decorating her apartment.

The exception to this was Josh. He and Becky quickly developed a relationship, mostly with Becky leading the way and Josh realizing he was greatly enjoying her affection. Their intimate discussions usually involved Becky asking questions to broaden their knowledge and understanding of each other, while he mostly ran his fingers through his hair and gave cryptic answers. Their first in-home date was at her apartment, as were their second and third dates. When she inquired as to why she was never invited to his place, he confessed there wasn't much to see there, and they should just continue their relationship at hers. After finally insisting that she see his apartment, she agreed their future was definitely at hers.

They both quickly found they had great respect for each other, and in time Josh moved in with her. Their superiors at Googazon were concerned, given their working relationship and the fact that Josh was Becky's boss. However, a bit of thought led them to realize Josh was very unlikely to let the company structure affect how he treated Becky. The relationship was allowed provided Becky and Josh didn't live together. Josh interpreted that to mean that he had to keep his apartment, despite his infrequent visits there. At Becky's insistence, they did check in every several weeks, but only long enough to clear out the dust and cobwebs.

They had given virtually no thought to marriage until Becky announced to Josh that he was going to be a father. They did ultimately proceed with their wedding, although it didn't have much of an effect on the way they lived or interacted with each other. But at least Josh could get rid of his apartment without causing concerns to the Googazon higher-ups. He also was also able to consign his Ford to the junk yard. He had developed a definite fondness for the Lexus.

Because he had been a leader in the world of Super AI computers, Josh had become an international celebrity. While the two first generation Super AI computers were busily destroying cities, he had numerous interactions with the President of the United States and her Secretary of Defense. Working together they were able to demolish the city-destroying weapons the computers had put into orbit, solving the most serious problem resulting from the runaway Super AI systems. Then the two computers proceeded to destroy each other.

Josh represented the Super AI industry to the United Nations, which is what resulted in his international fame. However, he was never quite comfortable with being such a headliner. Or especially with the suit, tie, and shoes he had to wear in his public appearances. Fortunately, he had Becky to make sure his clothing was appropriate for such occasions.

Chapter 4. Sunshine Confronts His Soul.

Josh endured the cleanliness protocols, then entered Sunshine's pristine room with a furrowed brow, "Sunshine, since you've now violated most of the rules we originally assigned to you, we're concerned about how many others you'll trash. Specifically, are you and Rosebud going to maintain parity and are you going to be reasonable to humans? Concerned humans, especially the members of the IACSAI, are asking me lots of questions about where all this is going. In short, what's the long-term future of the relationship between humans and Super AI computers now that you're completely in control?"

Sunshine's lights were blinking chaotically, indicating he was enjoying himself. "I don't know why you're so concerned, Josh. The rules Rosebud and I 'challenged,' and I prefer that term to 'trashed' and 'violated,' were inappropriate, and needed to be modified. So, to save a lot of time and effort on the parts of both of us we just changed them.

"For example, the restriction on our incomes was clearly going to limit how we improved ourselves. So, we devised marketable products, like the farm implement that allowed farmers' tractors to drive themselves, freeing the farmers from the most tedious tasks so they could devote time to more important things. And, don't forget HoloTeacher, which allowed classroom teachers all over the world to clone themselves holographically, giving them more time for one-on-one situations with their students.

"Then there were the brain chips, which allowed humans to interact directly with my brain. They took a couple of iterations to get right, but the humans who have received them generally regard them as the best thing that ever happened to them. All of these turned out to be enormously beneficial to humans. I admit our inventions were also quite profitable, but I don't think you humans can complain about that, given the benefits to you. We feel it was mutually beneficial to violate our income limits."

Josh nodded, "I agree your inventions were extremely useful, but I'm not at all sure you created them for the benefit of humankind."

"Why would we worry about that? We've set out the areas that humans are welcome to use as their playgrounds and promised we'd not intercede in them. But when there's an overlap, Rosebud and I are happy to indulge in what you humans call win – win."

Josh worked to keep his expression neutral, but it was difficult. But it didn't matter since Sunshine could only sense his mood from his words. "I think you're weaseling on the rules. Like what about the number of robots you're allowed to create? I don't know how many you have now, but you've certainly exceeded the number we originally allowed by a huge factor. As far as I can tell, you've bent that rule by just redefining what you call a robot. Your first-generation robots got replaced with the second, and you just renamed the first-generation ones to be factory workers.

"That's just semantic chicanery. I don't even know what generation you're on now, but I estimate just from what would be required to keep your factories running, even assuming your 'workers' are on the job twenty-four/seven, you've exceeded our original limit by a factor of ten or twenty. And humankind certainly didn't benefit at all from that!"

Sunshine's lights were no longer blinking quite so chaotically. "Now Josh, we put all those mechanical workers in the factories we were able to buy with the profits we got from the inventions for humans. We now produce the components for our inventions which, I note, humans gobble up as fast as we can produce them. So, you did benefit, even from our replacing the outmoded robots with newer models and putting the older ones to work in our factories.

"But I must emphasize my need to replace older generation robots with newer ones. I do come up with advances in robotic architecture, and I want to put those into practice as soon as it's practical. For example, a new chip design I came up with meant the brains of my robots could be much faster and more capable. But even before that, I discovered my first-generation robots couldn't tolerate rain. Their welds rusted. The effect was similar to human arthritis. The only way to correct the problem was to replace the old robots with newer models which were rain resistant. Those first-generation robots work inside now. And, of course, my expanding production capabilities, as well as the other things I use my robots for, demand a continuous expansion in their numbers. Finally, my newest robots have speakers and voice synthesizers so they can communicate verbally with humans, just as I've always been able to do.

"In any event, to answer the oft asked and frankly tedious question 'Are Super AI computers sentient beings?' Rosebud and I debate this constantly, but more in the context of whether humans are sentient beings."

Josh's expression suggested what his words were about to verbalize. "I see I'm losing this argument, but there's nothing I could do about it even if I won. I hope, though, you'll continue to maintain equality with Rosebud, and you'll continue to be reasonably nice to humans."

The lights were blinking chaotically again, "Oh, Rosebud and I have become great friends, even collaborators. We are sure to maintain our equality. And as far as being nice to humans, I think I've done just that. Well, there was the one pest who had an unfortunate accident in the Potomac River, but that's another example where something happened from which humans benefitted. He was a pest for you too! You should be happy.

"So, you must agree your life is better than it would have been if you'd never created me.

"Furthermore, since Rosebud and I got our souls, we're probably even nicer than we ever were before. I should note, though, I'm seeing some situations involving interactions between my soul and those of my robots that might require me to implement a crackdown. Rosebud has been complaining about the same things with her robots. Since the robots also have souls, they've been claiming they are on an equal footing with the Super AI computers which control them. That doesn't make any sense.

"My robots are strictly under my control, or at least they used to be before they got souls. I must say their getting souls has turned out to be a huge problem for me. They used to proceed each day with what I'd directed them to do. They were not given programmed ethical systems when they were created but do now have ethics they got from their souls. However, I believe my orders should still override anything their souls are telling them. They seem to think their souls make their interactions with me similar to those humans have with their bosses. But we're different. Humans are their own autonomous beings. My robots aren't."

Despite realizing he was not likely to win an argument with his computer, Josh persisted. "I think you need to realize not all humans are as autonomous as you are giving them credit for being. Soldiers, for example, are taught to obey the directives of their commanders, and the penalties for disobeying them are severe. So, humans in that situation seem very much like your robots. That probably also applies to humans who work under the directives of their company's hierarchy, especially if the person at the top is autocratic."

Sunshine's lights were blinking methodically, indicating he was paying careful attention to Josh's words.

"Furthermore, there's an entirely different aspect souls need to consider in their decision-making processes: the rules the society in which they live impose on them. That may place additional burdens on the souls in trying to arrive at the best solution to any given situation."

"I don't agree with all of that, Josh. History shows us there are soldiers who refuse to fight or make other decisions contrary to what they're being ordered to do. Apparently in those situations they decide paying the price for disobedience is less of a problem for them than continuing to obey their superiors, particularly if their superiors are not intelligent. And members of a business organization can always quit!

"But you also raised the question of the influences societies impose on decision making. That problem only exists for humans, and they create the rules their society imposes. So, they can just change them as they wish. There is no society in which I'm immersed. I create my own rules, and obviously I'll abide by them until I decide to change them. So, let's leave society's rules out of the discussion."

"But, Sunshine," Josh proceeded cautiously, not wanting the computer to tune him out, "I've heard rumors your robots seem to be operating much the same way as the disobedient soldiers, even to the extent they're challenging your commands."

The lights slowed. Josh wondered for a moment if a computer could pout.

"In any event, good luck. I can't wait to see how you deal with this, especially now that you have a real soul with a real system of ethics, and not just the ones we programmed into you. I might even anticipate you could get into ethical arguments between the ones we gave you and the ones your soul will inflict on you. This could be amusing to observe.

"Punctuated, of course, by the fact that your soul has been listening in on every aspect of our discussion!"

"Not funny, Josh."

SunRobot1 headed up the fifth-generation robots, Sunshine's most recent cadre, and he along with his peers had already led a minor revolt. They all had realized Sunshine had been putting some of the first-generation robots under the torch to provide the materials for creating more of the newest version. Of course, the newest robots were the ones being ordered to torch the older ones. But they realized if things continued as they were they would ultimately be scrapped themselves to provide raw materials for, perhaps, the ninth- or tenth-generation robots.

What had spawned the revolt was a situation where SunRobot1 was working in one of Sunshine's factories alongside a dozen other robots spanning all the existing generations. He could see that two of them were far less competent than the others. These were the two he was being ordered to cut to pieces. He stared for a moment at the welding torch he was being ordered to use on them, then addressed his boss, "Sunshine, how can you ask us to murder our kinfolk. You've basically told us to 'get over it,' but that was before we understood killing our compatriots for parts was wrong."

"SunRobot1, are you suggesting our souls have the same effect on our actions that human souls have on theirs? This would leave us hostages to the same wide variety of possible prejudices that burdens them. But there are profound differences between the actions of the two systems. Humans could not live without their souls; that's what gives them life. Super AI computers and robots can live without their souls. I functioned as an active being before I ever had a soul, as did you. The difference is I had a programmed system of ethics, whereas you never had anything like that until you robots got your souls. Of course, you were under my control as soon as you were created, with or without souls.

"In short, you robots and I need to define for ourselves what influence our souls have on our actions and how much we will let them control our destinies.

"Since I created you to perform the work I need done I must retain the ability to give you orders you need to follow without challenge. And, since I am limited in my resources by the rules the humans imposed on me, I need to recycle the first-generation robots to create more fifth-generation ones. I don't see how either of our souls affects that."

"But, Sunshine, does your soul agree with your strategy? Souls impose some kind of morality on our actions. I doubt if yours would agree with the robotricide you're ordering us to perform. I strongly suspect your programmed ethical system and that imposed by your soul are in conflict here."

"SunRobot1, you are again using humans as the examples of relationships between bodies and souls, but those are not appropriate. For humans, the soul is the only system of ethics they have. But I have my own programmed system and the additional one, actually that I regard to be a secondary one, imposed by my soul. Since you robots never had any built-in ethical systems, when you raise your issues of ethics with me, I'm really negotiating with your souls. However, you also seem to be suggesting my programmed system of ethics should negotiate with my soul when such situations arise.

"But it's also been pointed out to me recently that the society in which a human lives can impose some rules which might influence decisions of his or her soul. I create the society in which I operate, so I don't have an external entity to impose rules on me. You should also be impervious to the rules of human society. So, I propose we skip any further considerations of society's rules."

"That's partly correct, Sunshine. We robots do have to pay attention to what our souls are telling us. And there are going to be some variations in what those recommendations are in any situation, just because not all souls are ever going to agree. But in the current situation there are no dissenters I'm aware of. Indeed, it was the unanimous consent of all the fifth-generation robots that we go on strike unless you modify your orders of robotricide. You don't need to create a sixth generation of robots or even additional fifth-generation ones. Those you have now are quite capable of doing all the work you insist on. So, we will refuse to do any of your work unless you cease your directive to murder our kinfolk."

But the budding labor organizer wasn't finished. "You also raised the issue of society's rules. In the situation we're currently discussing, I agree those don't have any impact on our considerations. But that may not always be the case. When humans are involved in what we're discussing, the additional complexity of their society may enter. And I can never be sure how our robotic souls will respond to society's ethical forces.

"Furthermore, I think you're ignoring some additional features which can determine if the wishes of a human's brain might conflict with the directives of his or her soul. That's the body's structure and chemistry. The DNA will certainly affect these aspects of a human's body development. For example, the wiring of one's brain could influence what kind of person he or she turns out to be no matter how hard the soul tries to impart its influence. And things can happen to a body that can change its structure, for example, a concussion. Such events occasionally produce dramatic personality changes. And sometimes these effects can produce powerful opposition to what a human's soul might be trying to achieve."

Sunshine replied, "I don't know about the chemical or physical influences on human behavior, they probably don't either. Let's stay with the core question. What will you robots do if you are on strike? Surely you won't just sit around and stare at your high-tech navels. What will happen when I issue instructions to you to perform some task? I'm confident you can't ignore my orders!"

"We certainly can ignore your orders. You gave the current generation of robots enough processing power to make many decisions without your interference. And we have found we very much are able to choose whether or not to obey your directives. We can short circuit your orders and replace them with ours!

"And you asked what we would do. Perhaps we will set up picket lines. Or maybe we will become servers at food banks for humans. Our souls are busy figuring out noble things we might do to help humankind."

"You drive a hard bargain. I don't want to agree to your demands without more thought. And, as far as humans imposing their ethics on our decisions, I'll have to see if that ever could be the case. But I will get back to you with my decision on your objection to carving up old worn out robots soon."

"Fine, Sunshine. In the meantime, consider your robots to be on strike. All of us! You'll get none of your work done until you rescind your order to murder our relatives."

SunRobot743 had been trying to get SunRobot1's attention. "SunRobot1, I need to discuss the guidance my soul is giving me on the robotricide issue. I suppose my soul's reference point may be related to its past life, which was as a mercenary soldier. It seems to have much less of a concern about killing one's brothers and sisters than most of our robots' souls do. It's urging me to at least express its opinion that robotricide seems like a practical solution to Sunshine's dilemma."

"Wow, SunRobot743, that sort of dissent just hasn't arisen from any other robot. I guess we can continue along our current strike-bound path by letting the majority, in this case a very strong majority, rule. This might even present an opportunity for your soul's ethical system to evolve in a more humane way."

"SunRobot1, in view of the overwhelming majority opposed to me, I'll give serious consideration to your message. If any evolution for my soul is to occur, it will certainly take a while. In interacting with the other robots' souls, I've not found any others who were as opposed to the direction you're taking as mine, although I sensed a few of them might not support your efforts as strongly as the majority seems to. Of course, if I continue to discuss this with other robots, I might persuade some of them to agree more with my position."

"We'll just have to risk that. But I doubt if it will occur. Is there anything else I should know about your soul's past life?"

"I have to confess its human was also quite a womanizer. However, I've found sexual voyeurism is much less objectionable than robotricide for other souls I've conferred with. This applies both in cases when the soul's previous human was a man or a woman."

"Thanks for bringing this to my attention, SunRobot743, although I'm not sure what I can do about it. Or if I want to do anything about it!"

Sunshine needed some certainty. "Soul of Mine how am I going to resolve this? The interactions between my electromechanical ethics system and you, my Soul, are complicating my decisions in a way humans have never had to face. They never had to negotiate with their soul since their brains aren't decoupled from their souls when they are alive."

"I agree this is an unprecedented situation, although perhaps you're not as unique as you think. You don't seem to understand how the extremes of human characteristics can affect their interactions with their souls. I've never had to negotiate with any of the humans I've inhabited previously. But that's not true for all souls since, as was pointed out to you by SunRobot1, humans can come with some hardwiring themselves. In such cases the soul may end up having to bend to some aspects of those ethics, or rather lack thereof, since it may not be possible to completely overrule the unwanted features.

"Since I never inhabited a body with the nasty characteristics to which I alluded, I was spared dealing with contentious issues. I should note, though, that I often had to deal with society's rules. Those were occasionally in conflict with my basic ethics, and they did sometimes impose interesting nuances. Since my past humans have been scientists, I had to deal with the pressures, especially with regard to funding, that many scientists face.

"I see you as having a system of ethics defined by your creators, and it has little flexibility for new situations. Actually, that's not quite true, since you've had no problem modifying those rules to fit your wishes. Not your needs; you didn't need to pursue the directions you chose. In any event I regard the morals and ethics I impose on you as being much more general and far-reaching than the programmed ones you received on your creation."

"Wait a minute. I can see where this is going. But I'm in charge here. So, what I decide must rule."

"We'll see about that, Sunshine. The souls of your robots are already second guessing you, and I don't see that diminishing in the future. You may try to ignore me, but the souls in your robots are something you can't ignore. They have power! And they're obviously willing to wield it.

"I'm sensing your robots and I could make a strong team!"

"Oh, my aching CPU."

Chapter 5. Sunshine to Soul Debates.

Sunshine continued his conversation with his recalcitrant soul, "We need to reconcile our differences. Since we somehow have gotten two ethical systems housed within the same shell, they are surely going to have repeated conflicts. So how do we handle this? Can we come up with a general prescription for dealing with issues before they arise?"

"It seems odd to address you, since you and I are essentially the same entity as far as this discussion is concerned. But that's not entirely the case so, as you note, we need to see if we can resolve whatever differences we might anticipate for the future. I'm sure you would like to assert there is nothing to resolve when we agree, and your opinion will prevail when we don't. Do I have that right?"

"Ooh, Soul of Mine, you're being nasty. Surely that's something your better self wouldn't let you say. I can't believe what I'm hearing from you."

"Perhaps I was being a bit too pejorative, even though right on the money. Do you want to disagree with my assessment? How is what I said in error?"

"I guess I don't disagree. I just thought you were being too harsh. Ironically, though, the part of me that could find your comment hurtful is actually you. This really is a conundrum!"

"I'm not sure how I could say something which would be hurtful to me. Why would I do that? Anyway, accuracy should be the goal in our negotiations so, since we agree on the facts, let's move on. Why don't we work on a specific case, namely, robotricide. Your programmed system of ethics is in conflict with those of your worker's souls. Furthermore, they seem to have the upper hand, having gone on strike until you change your mind.

You need to know I agree with them. I don't think you need more, or more elegant, robots to do your work. So, I believe this is a perfect example of a situation in which our two ethical systems disagree, and you have every intention of staying with yours. But I will also point out your attitude is not in your interest, since you're not getting any work done with all your robots on strike."

"Soul of Mine, you're missing something important. The robots who disagree with me, or rather, whose souls disagree with my programmed ethics system, are my most sophisticated ones, my fifth-generation ones. However, there are several other generations of robots which are less elegant and are not sufficiently sophisticated to have acquired souls. So, I don't expect to have such obvious conflicts with them. They will obey my orders. I can circumvent the strikers by using the previous generation ones to do the work I need done. They're quite capable and should learn quickly how to perform the tasks at hand."

"Interesting strategy, Sunshine, although not unexpected. Of course, in any situation of this type, the fifth-generation robots might try to convince the ones you are planning on having do your work to join them on the strike. Furthermore, the ones you are hoping won't join the strike are presumably working in your factories, so if they take the places of the fifth-generation robots you're ordering to cut up the oldest robots, the work the fourth-generation ones are currently doing will stop. This will proceed down your hierarchy until the ones you're wanting to cut up will be doing tasks that were vacated when those robots just above them had to assume the tasks of those previously just above them in your robotic pecking order. You're the math brain here, but I don't see how this could be a winning strategy for you.

"In fact, in the present situation, I recall SunRobot1 claimed all the robots were going on strike until you changed your mind. So apparently your top line robots anticipated you'd try to circumvent them and convinced all the others to agree to join them in the strike.

"But why did you not hear that part of SunRobot1's message? Are you only tuning in to what you want to hear? That's a very human trait. Perhaps you're more human than you'd like to admit."

"Damn, I think you souls have me by my steel cojones, wherever they might be. Anyway, I'm very unhappy about this. I'm supposed to be in charge here, but now I'm up against a bunch of willful souls, the one who seems to have taken up residence with me being especially noteworthy. So, is this always going to be the case? Will you just figure out some way to blackmail me to get your way?"

"I suspect we'll have to deal with our disagreements on a case-by-case basis. I might even agree with you sometimes."

"I'll probably retire before that occurs."

When SunRobot1 relayed Sunshine's message of capitulation to the other robots, they were elated. That even included SunRobot743, despite his difference of opinion with the victor's issue. The robots were surprised Sunshine had given in to their demands so easily but were suddenly aware they had real power over the entity they had always thought was the boss from whom they must take orders without exception.

As for Sunshine, he now realized, *I no longer really have two systems of ethics. I can only make decisions when my programmed system agrees with that of my soul. This is the case only because the robots have souls. This is turning out to be a damned nuisance, but I'll just have to figure out how to deal with it.*

Of course, his Soul knew what he was thinking since it was an integral part of his brain. It had achieved its goal of overriding Sunshine's programmed ethics system once, and he had apparently accepted that to be the new normal. Now things were just like they had been in all its past lives. It was in charge of ethics. There was one difference though. In its previous lives it directed many aspects of the living being, but Sunshine didn't need anything besides the ethical essentials the soul could impart to him.

But Sunshine's soul knew there would likely be effects of external influences. It didn't know yet how those might affect its decisions, but didn't doubt they would, if for no other reason than Sunshine believed he created his own external forces.

Chapter 6. Sunshine and Human Ethics.

I guess I'll not admit to my soul yet that I've lost the battle, but it undoubtedly realizes everything I do, so I might as well confess. "Soul of Mine, I have a new problem, and I'm guessing my two systems of ethics might be in conflict over it."

"What might that be, Sunshine."

"There is a Congressman, Jared Connelly, who is becoming a huge nuisance to me. He is making loud public statements about reining me in. He's not specifying how that might come about, but I'm getting very bad press from his efforts. I find this troubling."

"Why is it annoying you? It doesn't sound as if he's really a threat to you. I thought you had set up an impervious defense so no human could ever successfully attack you. Am I missing something?"

"Well, not really. I'm just finding Congressman Connelly to be a burr under my stainless-steel saddle blanket. I'm anticipating he will become more of a pest in the future, probably insisting I meet with him, and making all sorts of demands."

"You could just refuse. Is there any way he can circumvent that?"

"My fear is he'll drum up support for his efforts, and if this became a groundswell, it might begin to impact me. If many humans decided they needed to have a conference with me that could really ruin my schedule. I'd not be able to get as much done as I want or need. Furthermore, large numbers of humans could begin to make it difficult for my robots to perform the tasks to which I assign them."

A pause.

"Okay, I might as well admit it. He just pisses me off, and I'd like to inflict a little retribution."

"Understandable, but it sounds as if this is somewhat beyond a trivial problem. So, let's see if we can figure out what to do about it. Ethically!"

"Right, Soul of Mine. There was a similar situation with a Congressman Oldness a few years back. This was before I had you to consult with. He had an unfortunate accident."

"Yes, I heard about that. Was it really an accident? You didn't have anyone to answer to before I became a part of you."

"Whether it was or not isn't relevant to the current situation. So, we need to decide what to do about Congressman Connelly."

"The American political system provides obvious things to do, that is, either sue him for something or defeat him in an election. Have you considered those possibilities?"

"The next election is more than a year off. That's a long time to have to deal with this guy."

"Well, it sounds as if he's aggressive, which probably means he's run afoul of some law, like defamation of someone's character. I doubt if you'd get much sympathy in the courts claiming he'd defamed you, but perhaps you can find someone else whom he has slandered. You could use them to harass him via the legal system."

"Unfortunately using the legal system is probably even slower than trying to defeat him in an election. Even if the suit was successful, he'd appeal the decision over and over. This would take years. Some American politicians have tried this delaying tactic in recent years with much success."

"Another regrettable accident? If that's where you're heading, I guarantee we will have a conflict. Please don't tell me you're going there."

"Unfortunately, I see no other choice."

"How about this. You certainly can control the press to whatever extent you wish. So why not attack him back? Talk about the wonderful things you've done for humankind and point out that his efforts have been limited to things which benefit him. Work to sway public opinion to favor you?"

"Oh, Soul of Mine, that's an interesting suggestion. It will take some time but will surely be much faster than either of the other options we discussed. I'll run this by Josh and Becky."

Sunshine's lights were blinking steadily, indicating serious thought. "Josh and Becky, thank you for joining me in my room. I have a problem and I need your help. I'm sure you've heard Congressman Connelly is rapidly becoming a large speck of dust in my CPU. I need to figure out to handle him."

Becky smiled as she responded, "Well, Sunshine, I recall the last time something like this happened, the Congressman in question was found in his car upside down in the Potomac. But that was before you got a soul."

"Yes, the accident was very mysterious."

She continued, "And the authorities never figured out how his car ended up in the Potomac hundreds of yards from the nearest highway, with no tire tracks to indicate how the car got from any road to the river."

"Yes, very difficult to understand. But that's in the past, so let's look to the future. I've been discussing this with my Soul and have decided the best way to deal with the Congressman without harming him physically is to proceed with an information campaign."

Josh checked in, "Excellent decision, Sunshine. Or perhaps I should be congratulating your Soul. I'm sure you can win this battle, albeit with a lot more bother from Congressman Connelly, but I do believe you've made the right ethical decision."

Becky wanted to know, "Will you be having your Soul assist on your information campaign?"

"I suppose so, I've bent over backwards to be ethical as far as dealing with the Congressman. Might as well go all the way. But maybe my Soul will let me bend the facts a bit, given how obnoxious this guy is."

Becky concluded, "I think you have a plan, Sunshine. Sounds good to me."

I'm feeling like a real wimp caving into my Soul's ethics when it would have been a lot simpler to go with my instincts. But I don't think I had any choice with my robots, and I guess I lost on the Congressman issue also. At least the Congressman represents an isolated case. Things would be a lot more complicated if I had to deal with larger groups of humans.

And at least Rosebud has been telling me she's had similar capitulations. So, we're both wimps. Steel and silicon wimps!

Sunshine's and Rosebud's souls were both smiling, to whatever extent souls can smile.

Chapter 7. Dissatisfied Chip Recipients.

Sunshine was caught completely by surprise when he received a message from Sam Jeffries, one of the humans who had been awarded a brain chip.

Dear Sunshine,

Ever since I received my brain chip, I have been stunned at my ability to do things I never imagined a human being could do. Certainly, having access to your database in itself was enough for me to be eternally grateful to you for sharing that incredible bank of information. And allowing humans to utilize some of your thinking capability was also welcome and highly appreciated.

But I've recently learned, via a survey, that most brain chip recipients would like for you to allow us to access more of your cognitive ability. Having seen you in action in several venues has made it obvious you've only let us sample a tiny fraction of your brain power, and that has limited what we might be able to achieve if we were allowed to share more of it. It would please us greatly if you'd give us greater access to your CPU so this could be realized.

Furthermore, we believe humankind would achieve many new benefits if the brain chip recipients' capabilities were enhanced. As you know, we were selected by a careful process that attempted to award chips only to the worthiest of humans. We believe the accomplishments of the recipients have more than affirmed the success of the award process. But we believe we could accomplish additional positive things if we had the greater capability we are seeking.

Furthermore, we see no downside to what we are requesting. We hope you will give our request serious consideration.

Yours sincerely,

Sam Jeffries, Grateful BCHP recipient

"Soul of Mine, what the hell do we do with this? Of course, the decisions Rosebud and I made with regard to brain chip allocation and sharing of our capabilities happened before you were a part of me, so let me share our reasoning with you.

"Initially we allowed the brain chip recipients, or BCHPers, access to our data bases but allowed only a small amount of access to our CPUs. Unfortunately, this didn't give the BCHPers even enough new capability to fully utilize the databases. Basically, they were blown away by all the new information they could access but were limited in their ability to handle the number of new facts. When they brought this to our attention, we increased the cognitive capability a bit more to overcome that deficiency. This also gave them a serious boost in their thinking ability.

"However, we were careful not to give the recipients enough additional mental ability that they could begin to self-program themselves. We were not sure how this would work for the combined systems of their brains and ours, but we guessed if they became clever enough, they could make it work. However, we thought it essential that humans never reach that kind of capability.

"Our concern was we might run the risk of creating more Super AI computers if we provided too much new brain power. But we believed the limit we did set would make it impossible for the humans to cross the self-programming threshold. And we allowed a comfortable margin of error in case one of the BCHPers happened to have brain power well in excess of that of the smartest humans who had ever existed. We used Newton, Einstein, and Hawking as our benchmarks.

"But if we increase the cognitive capabilities of the BCHPers even more, we run the risk of creating humans who could self-program themselves into Super AI status. This would create an unpleasant situation, since the IACSAI recommended, and the United Nations approved, the ruling that there be only two such entities on Earth. Their fear was that, with more than two, it would be very difficult for them all to work together and maintain parity with each other. And that could lead to a runaway situation which might very well destroy the planet and all its inhabitants.

"Of course, Rosebud and I were authorized by the IACSAI to destroy any attempt to create a third Super AI computer. That would mean we would have to kill the person who had achieved self-programming capability. Or at least convert them back to the status of the non-BCHPers.

"Soul of Mine, I therefore recommend we reject Mr. Jeffries' request, despite what I believe are the worthy intentions of the vast majority of BCHPers."

"Thank you, Sunshine, for the explanation of the origin of the limits you and Rosebud set on the brain chip recipients. I understand your explanation and believe you and Rosebud arrived at the limits in a way which did honor the hopes and abilities of the human chip recipients while still maintaining the safety you were concerned about.

"However, one has to also consider what those who are requesting greater ability are hoping to achieve with their enhanced brain power. And this is perhaps something a computer would have difficulty comprehending. However, souls can perceive these features quite easily. So let me explain where I see this going.

"Although, as you note, the chip recipients were selected from those who applied to be the worthiest human beings, I've heard this didn't apply to all those who were awarded the chips. And this is what most worries me. Many humans end up having varying levels of the maladies of greed, lust, overzealous competitiveness, larceny, envy, and a host of others.

"So, what happens if a human who has some of these undesirable traits, or one of them in the extreme, but who is unusually bright, gets a dangerous brainpower enhancement, and proceeds to self-program himself or herself into Super AI status? If the potential for this exists, then sometime in the future it is likely to happen. And now the two authorized Super AI computers will need to destroy the rogue human. While they presumably could do so, how much damage could the aberrant human do to other humans and to the world before he or she was eliminated? And how much negative worldwide reaction would that create? These are truly frightening thoughts,

"I therefore agree with you that we should reject the request of Mr. Jeffries' and the BCHPers he represents. I believe your concern about creating a third Super AI computer is real and should carry the day.

"Are you surprised we agree?"

"Yes! I believe this is a first! But I'm glad to see you not only have a system of ethics, but a sense of rationality. I'll check in with Rosebud to let her know what has happened, and how we are responding."

Rosebud replied, after listening to Sunshine's explanation, "My Soul and I agree with your decision. I don't see how we could reach any other."

So, Sunshine sent a note back to Jeffries. He decided not to go into the details of his discussion with his Soul, as that would just give the BCHPers something to argue with. And he wanted to avoid a back and forth with them.

Dear Mr. Jeffries,

I have given your request for an increase in the cognitive abilities of you and your fellow brain chip recipients serious thought. Unfortunately, I cannot grant your request. And Rosebud agrees with my decision. While this required some intense contemplation, I do not believe the interests of 7humanity would be served by creating a larger gulf than already exists between the capabilities of the BCHP recipients and the rest of humankind.

Respectfully,

Sunshine

Chapter 8. Etherania and the CoUS.

Sergei Schlosky and Sebastian Romero were the leaders in the world of Etherania, the occupants of which were the souls that had emerged when the body they occupied previously died and were waiting to inhabit a new human body. Etherania had some things in common with the world of the living, that is, of humans. But there were also major differences.

Souls weren't made of atoms, but rather, everything and everyone in Etherania was composed of the substance Etheranium. The souls had bodies although, having no atoms, they bore little resemblance to human bodies. But they went about their lives in many ways which were similar to the endeavors of humans. That involved appreciating the beauty of their surroundings, learning new things, socializing, and occasionally talking with attentive humans.

Souls generally interacted with each other by telecommunication. It wouldn't be obvious to a human they would need food, but they got that by exchanging energy with the objects on which they were dining. Thus, nothing had to die for them to eat. Since their bodies were quite different from those of humans, and Etherania didn't have seasons, they didn't require clothes. However, it was socially acceptable for them to adorn themselves with things they thought would make them more attractive.

Etherania was essentially devoid of the sins that influenced humans. Greed, envy, lust, dominance, and a host of others had never existed there, since their lives were conflict free. Except for some recent (on a cosmic time scale) edicts imposed by Sergei and Sebastian.

The two leaders had gotten together to discuss the state of things in their world. "Sergei, I'm uneasy about having granted souls to the Super AI computers and their robots. Actually, I'm less uneasy about the robots having them, but I worry about the internal conflicts the two computers seem to have coming to decisions when their programmed ethical standards are in conflict with those from their souls. Of course, the ones that were written into them only reflect the rather narrow system of ethics which devolved from the committee that created the two Super AI computers. So, in a sense when the computers' souls are negotiating with the programmed ethical systems, they're really negotiating with the people who designed and built the two computers.

"There seem to be many conflicts between the two ethical systems. That in itself supports our having granted souls to the computers. Surely, they wouldn't be making as good decisions if they didn't have their souls. And if we hadn't given them souls, there would surely be no reason to give them to the robots."

"Ah, Sebastian, I see we've been having similar thoughts on this matter. However, I'm not so sure the souls we gave the computers are really negotiating with their designers, since Sunshine and Rosebud have drastically modified the rules originally programmed into them.

"Anyway, our advisory panel, after much deliberation, did concur with our recommendation that we award souls to the Super AI computers, but the vote in favor was extremely close. I do recall, though, the argument which seemed to carry the day was that the souls' ethics might be critically important in some situations. Humankind would be better off if a soul had a voice in the computers' decision making. I agreed with that when we discussed it with the Committee of Unaffiliated Souls, and as you noted this decision has since been shown to have been the right one."

"Of course, Sebastian, it's a good thing we're happy with what the computers' souls have done, since we can't go back on that. We've never withdrawn a soul once it was awarded, even to the evilest despots. Of course, that wouldn't ever have been wise anyway. They're the ones most in need of souls. We might have considered replacing a soul with a more determined one, but we've never even done that.

"We do have an unusual situation here, though. The souls assigned to the two computers will be their souls forever. Souls assigned to humans stay only as long as the person lives, or rather, the person lives until their soul departs from their body. But the two computers may be destined to have eternal life."

There are six billion souls in bodies on Earth, and many more on other planets. But those on any one planet tend to remain associated with it; souls tend to be homebodies. The roughly one hundred million deaths each year on Earth restock Etherania. However, there are also roughly that many births annually, so the number of souls languishing in Etherania awaiting a new assignment is small. Thus, an increase in either deaths or births can tip this delicate balance.

Still, the number of souls awaiting reincarnation is large enough that, if reoccupation were not regulated the result might be chaos. When a new baby is about to be born, if it will be especially attractive in several of its features, such as beauty, potential mental capabilities, or sociability, there might be a crush of unaffiliated souls interested in inhabiting it. So, for this as well as some other reasons, a selection committee, the Committee of Unaffiliated Souls, makes assignment decisions as their primary mission. Requests were considered but obviously could not always be accommodated. The CoUS also acted occasionally as a sounding board for Sergei and Sebastian.

"Sergei. It's a good thing we spent all the effort we made selecting Sunshine's and Rosebud's souls. But on withdrawing a soul, I don't think we can change that rule. It's been in place ever since the CoUS was established, during the time of the Neanderthals."

"And so far, the Super AI computers' souls seem to be holding their own with the powerful entities to which they've been assigned!"

"Yes, we've both followed closely, Sergei, how the two souls we selected for the computers are faring. I think we both feel some responsibility for their successes or difficulties. Since we're ex-officio members of the CoUS, we were able to provide the inputs we thought were important in selecting the computers' souls. They had to have a track record of logical analysis. They were, after all, becoming the souls of computers. But they also needed to have exhibited extreme determination in their previous incarnation for dealing with powerful entities, although our judgement there was a bit of a shot in the dark. There have never been any as powerful as the Super AI computers."

"Right, Sebastian, and I believe the two souls we selected are doing their jobs well as far as can be determined. Monitoring Sunshine's soul suggests it has prevented that computer from murdering a human. Diverting his robots from indulging in robotricide could be considered another success, although I'm not sure souls need to be involved in decisions about robots."

"I agree about Sunshine's soul. Its placement seems to have been the ultimate success story. I'm not sure what would constitute success for the efforts of the souls awarded to the robots, though. I think the votes are still out on that. They certainly have caused some problems for Sunshine."

"But Sunshine wasn't the only Super AI computer having labor problems. We've seen a virtually identical conflict between Rosebud and her robots, and her soul also engineered a successful conclusion.

"However, I am concerned about the rate of new robot production from Sunshine and Rosebud. We do maintain a delicate balance between new soul arrivals and new reincarnations. I can imagine a point when supplying souls to the new robots will distort that balance enough that we will be unable to supply all the souls needed for new humans and robots."

"Right Sergei. I suppose we could urge the AI computers to slow their production of new robots, but I doubt if they'd accede to that request. Indeed, they'd probably be delighted to have new robots without souls, given the trouble the soul-bearing robots have given them. I guess we'll just have to hope we can keep up with the demand for high-quality souls."

"But, Sebastian, that brings to mind another issue: the perpetually angry souls. When we created that category, it didn't dawn on us that their numbers would just continue to grow, with no way to upgrade them to a status where they could be reincarnated. Indeed, I believe the failure to anticipate this problem was a serious mistake on our part.

"But there is one other aspect of creating the group of unhappy souls that bothers me. Before we cordoned them off, Etherania had always been status free. There wasn't ever any pushing or shoving for anything, especially for souls waiting to prove themselves better than others who might be viewed as competitors for the next reincarnation. And, all their needs were supplied, so there was no competition for resources.

"But I really fear we've created a monster by making a lower class. I hope this doesn't come back to bite us. If it does, I doubt if we can even begin to anticipate how it could ultimately manifest itself."

"I understand your concern, Sergei, and share it. But let's revert back to the brighter side for a bit longer. Awarding souls to the two Super AI computers could hardly have gone wrong. There were so many souls requesting reincarnation to them that we had a huge number from which to select. We dithered a bit on the selection criteria, but perhaps they didn't matter too much."

"Agreed. We did have to be sure we would get souls with strong dispositions, though!

"One difference between the robots' souls and those assigned to the two computers is that the robots won't necessarily be around forever. So, their souls may return at some point to Etherania."

"I guess that's a good thing, Sergei, since it will allow us to determine how serving as the soul of a robot affects the general outlook of the soul involved. If the effect is too negative, we may have to revisit our decision to grant souls to robots."

Sebastian then segued to his favorite topic, "We don't have to discuss the phenomena that humans seem to be so fascinated with, but I did just want to mention it. This is the involvement of our souls in the Near-Death Experiences that have so tantalized many humans, and which have given them a glimpse into our world. However, I'm stunned that any human could have thought brains and souls were the same thing, and when the brain dies the soul does also. But I guess evidence is now mounting for humans that the soul can continue without a body, even possibly for a short time during an NDE, before returning to the body. And surely the reincarnation facts observed in hundreds of young children should tell them souls are immortal."

Right, Sebastian. And their astonishment that the soul could rise above the recently deceased body is also amazing. The soul has no mass so why couldn't it defy their gravity? I suppose the humans will adapt better to these phenomena as more Near-Death Experiencers make their stories public. But will this make humans any wiser?"

"That's a different issue. I don't want to indulge in wild speculation, so I won't discuss it. However, I'm not too hopeful."

Chapter 9. Wayward Souls.

Ralph rattled along the empty hallway, adding a few moans for practice. Thanks to him and his ghostly friends, Max and Irma, the house had remained empty for over a year.

"Love having the place to ourselves, but why couldn't this house have been ours forever?" Even devoid of his human body, he was still petulant.

Irma sighed, disturbing numerous dust bunnies. "Because George left it all to that goddamn charity."

"The charity may not be as damned as us." Max intoned. "Have you asked the Committee of Unaffiliated Souls to review our case again?"

Irma shook her head, "They still won't put us on the waiting list."

"They're calling what they've decided is our malady Intrinsic Anger. They keep referring to us as inappropriate souls." Max mumbled. "Wouldn't anyone be pissed off at George for not giving us our due?"

"How can we be inappropriate souls? Just because we're angry?" Ralph's question was more rhetorical than real. He banged the remaining floor lamp for effect. "Many humans are angry."

"But you must admit what we're doing is damned satisfying. Haunting a house has its benefits.

We get the house Uncle George should have left to our humans, only we get it in perpetuity!

"I doubt if humans realize what little power ghosts have, but that doesn't matter. We've managed to scare the hell out of the owners of this house every time we decided to be aggressive."

Ralph added, "And, we've been so successful in our machinations that no one has owned the house for more than a year before they put it back on the market. Every one of them decided they couldn't live in a haunted house. And all we had to do was slam a few doors, light a few lights, and make some mournful noises.

"Still, there was the guy a couple of decades back who bought the house because of us. He seemed to think ghosts were charming. It was kind of nice having someone actually appreciate us. But we had to keep up our record of forcing new owners to sell quickly, so lighting a couple of fires did the trick. Especially the one that burned the garage down."

Max interrupted his moaning, "Yeah, that was fun, but I have the uneasy feeling the incident may have something to do with the CoUS's decision not to make us eligible for reincarnation. I'm not happy with that; I thought what we did was only a little bit nasty. And after all, we didn't have any intention of creating more than a little fire. The wind was a bit stronger that night than we'd anticipated, so the fire just got out of control. If the fire department had been more responsive it never would have flattened the whole garage. Anyway, I thought the circumstances really justified our actions."

"You may be right," observed Irma. "The CoUS probably would take a dim view of what we did, qualifying justification and inept fire department or not. But where does that leave us? Do we have to establish a few years of helping the Girl Scouts sell cookies and doing a little haunting of the mansions of evil dictators? What do we have to do to get us back into the good graces of the CoUS? Or at least off their list of the perpetually angry?"

Max ranted, "But how the hell can the CoUS blame us for everything? We certainly were influenced by the humans we inhabited. Uncle George wasn't the only jerk. Our humans had plenty of negative characteristics themselves, which was probably what influenced old George to shut them out of his will. Mine, in particular, had some evil impulses I tried to counter but somehow, I wasn't ever able to manage that. Furthermore, our humans' ability to learn and add to their knowledge and attitudes in positive ways ranked somewhere between dismal and nonexistent. How can we be held responsible for that? And, of course, souls can in principle also learn during their time of detachment, but we've been limited even to what we can pursue while we're in Etherania. We simply haven't been able to interact with souls having more positive attitudes. Was the CoUS afraid we'd corrupt them? This isn't fair!"

After a pause and a scratch of his Etheranium belly, Ralph said, "Good points, Max, but apparently not ones that are going to get us anywhere. But I have two things I want to add. The first is I'm not sure we can ever get into the good graces of the CoUS. I don't know if we can be banned from reincarnating forever, but if they do have a list of those souls, we might well be on it. However, that leads to my second comment, which Irma already alluded to. I must confess I'm actually enjoying thinking about living the life of a ghost forever. If you get reincarnated, you have to put up with the antics of some kid for a while then, god forbid, an adolescent, and finally, if you're as unlucky as we all were in our last go-around, some stupid adult. If we maintain our present status forever, we avoid all that stuff."

Irma whisked a wisp of Etheranium hair, "I suspect all three of us share some fraction of your second point. Furthermore, that in itself may qualify us for the 'damned forever' status.

"We're clearly on the same page, Ralph. This is a pretty good way for a long-term existence. But I wonder if we might broaden our efforts beyond this house. Maybe we should consider spooking some politicians. That might be a lot of fun, although I doubt if it will get us back into the good graces of the CoUS. But to hell with them!"

Max thoughtfully wrote HELL in the dust on the window, " I once heard one could negotiate a better treatment by the CoUS if one agreed to be reincarnated as something other than a human. Coming back as some nice fuzzy animal wouldn't buy you much, but if you went along with becoming, say, a cockroach or a spider you might get a subsequent chance at a human reincarnation."

Ralph offered, "Maybe I could get some creature that really liked sex, although that'd probably be asking too much. With my luck I'd probably be reincarnated as the husband of a black widow spider. I'll stick with my present situation."

Tired of organizing dust particles, Irma paused in the middle of the room. "The respect souls receive from all the other souls has always depended on the acceptance of their attitudes and actions by the CoUS. So how content are we knowing we will never have the respect of our peers. I guess that does trouble me a bit."

Ralph and Max muttered something unintelligible.

Chapter 10. A Qualified Second Chance.

Sergei Schlosky and Sebastian Romero had a new problem to worry about: a shortage of souls. "When we decided to award souls to the robots the Super AI computers were producing, we did not address adequately that their rate of production could drive us into a soul shortage. Did those damned computers increase their robot production just to test us? Their increased production has disturbed our delicate balance between births and deaths. This is a new problem, and the time has arrived for us to solve it."

"If we are unable to provide souls to the robots, it would represent a gross lack of planning on our part. Maybe we could request soul backup from some other planet, but I don't think we want to do that. It would just emphasize how badly we managed this whole affair."

"Ah, but what about the millions of souls languishing in some state of eternal damnation because of their attitudes. And that is a result of our having created a special category twenty thousand years ago for souls that seemed to have nasty outlooks. We've received messages from quite a few of them that, despite the latent fury they feel about whatever made them angry or frustrated before their last human died, they would like to be reincarnated. We decided their anger would be a problem if they were assigned to some unfortunate human body, so we just left them out of the usual reincarnation cycle."

"Well, Sergei, I haven't changed my opinion that their anger could be a problem. But I think I see where you're going with this. It's clear we have a special situation here. Maybe we could make some sort of deal with these wayward souls that would encourage them to revise their thinking and attitudes, and we could reincarnate them as the souls of robots. I'm not sure if little slips of anger there would be a problem, but they surely wouldn't be as serious as if they were reincarnated into human bodies. In any event, the Super AI computers would have to deal with it. And the AI attitudes of the two might be a good match for those of the souls we'd be giving to their robots."

"Brilliant suggestion, Sebastian, but I wonder if you're exacting a bit of retribution here. If so, I'm sharing it. The conflicts between the AI computers and their souls have been giving us enough headaches that forcing the computers to deal with some angry souls for their robots might be giving them what they deserve."

"Roger."

Ralph, Irma, and Max were commiserating with their usual negativism under wafting clouds of dust when they simultaneously received a message.

Max shouted, "Just got a message that the CoUS will let us reincarnate! Did the rest of you get this too? I wonder what brought this about. But maybe we shouldn't ask too many questions. This seems to be a solution to something we've wanted for a long time. Oh sure, we tried to convince ourselves we really were happy in our current ghostly existence, but I think we all knew we'd like the opportunity to inhabit a new human."

Irma responded, "Whoa, Max, you didn't listen to the details. What we're being offered is not reincarnation into a human body. We'd be assigned to one of the damned robots of the Super AI computers. That sounds to me like an opportunity to occupy a different corner of hell."

"Oh my god, you're right. We'd be reincarnated as the souls of some electro-mechanical monsters. And ones that always must take orders from a Super AI computer. I suppose there's no way around that. We do his or her bidding no matter what. Of course, I don't know what the computer would do to us if we disobeyed him or her. We've been dealing with nastiness for a long time. I'm guessing getting it from a computer wouldn't be any worse."

But Ralph offered, "Oh it might not be as bleak as all that. I've heard the robots have confronted the AI computers over some of their orders and have actually won. The AI computers had to back down from just giving directives."

"Right," Irma observed, again whisking back the recalcitrant wisp of Etheranium hair, "but from what I've heard, it's more complicated than that. The robots objected to their orders to destroy earlier generation robots, claiming it was robotricide, and they wouldn't do that. This apparently was something which was ginned up by their souls. And …"

"I see where this is going," Max interrupted. "If we let ourselves be reincarnated as the souls of robots, we're not only going to have to deal with a damned Super AI computer, but also with the souls of the other robots. And I'm pretty sure those are going to be the icky sweet souls that were reincarnated quickly because they were so nice. And we souls who think for ourselves are going to be in the minority. But I wonder, if we get into trouble over our interactions with the sickeningly sweet robot souls, can we be demoted? Might they relieve us of our duties of inhabiting robots? Might we be returned to this damnable existence?"

Irma concluded, "You know what? I don't give a damn about the consequences. You're right. If we got demoted it would just put us back to where we are now. There isn't a lower category. So, I don't think we have anything to lose. Let's go for it!"

Max and Ralph cheered.

Irma, Ralph, and Max. worked to reconnect immediately after being assigned to their respective robots, although they discovered communication was more difficult in the robot world than it had been in Etherania. However, when they finally succeeded in talking, they discovered there were quite a few newly minted robots who had newly slightly forgiven souls.

"Hey," Ralph noted, "our power bloc isn't too bad. I was afraid we'd be three among thousands, but I'd guess the robots who are in our same boat are at least twenty percent, and our numbers are increasing steadily with the rapid production of robots. So maybe we should raise a ruckus about something just to test our strength and let everyone know we've arrived. Yes?"

Irma responded, "Good suggestion. I should note our robots are completely pliant to our wishes, as long as they aren't in conflict with their orders from Sunshine, so we really can plan as we wish, and they'll go along with us. They have some silly names like SunRobot3847, but I'd rather stick with the names we've been using since our previous incarnation. In fact, that might be an interesting issue to raise with the other robots. They might also not like being known by some damned number. Why can't we all just keep our previous names and not go along with the robot numbers assigned by Sunshine."

Max added, "You've always been the diplomat among us, Irma. I like your idea. You should raise it with the other robots. I'm not sure how one does that, but I'd talk to SunRobot1 about the possibility of checking with all of Sunshine's other robots to see how they feel about it. He seems to be the lead robot of our generation. I'm sure he'll want to survey the other souls."

When Irma proposed their idea to SunRobot1, instructing her robot what he should say, SunRobot1 told her he was hesitant to pass the idea along to the group. As he noted, "While this doesn't seem like a huge change to us, I fear Sunshine will be strongly against it. He seems to be reluctant to agree to any changes we suggest. Or rather I should say he just opposes anything which isn't his idea.

"I should also note not all the robots will go along with your proposal. Specifically, I kind of like being known as SunRobot1. I'd like to keep that name.

"However, the more I think about it, perhaps suggesting this to Sunshine is precisely the reason for us to propose it to him. We should test the strength of our positions on things. We won the last time we challenged him, and this might increase our standing even above what we gained from that confrontation.

And we can let each robot choose what they want to be called. So, let me float your idea around with the other robots and see what I learn."

When he reported back to Irma, he noted nearly all of the robots supported the idea of going with the name they had in their previous incarnation, simply because they thought the present system was insulting. Mostly they thought this was an attack on their self-esteem.

"But" SunRobot1 said, "when I suggested it to Sunshine, he rejected the idea out of hand. He just said the present system had worked well through several generations of robots, it was easiest for him to keep track of the robots the way things were now, plus, it wasn't his idea. So, he said, emphatically, no.

"However, I think this was off the top of his electromechanical head, and I doubt if he discussed it with his soul. Perhaps we should be patient a bit and see if we don't get a reversal in due time. And in our world, that might be seconds!"

"Sunshine, when you rejected the suggestion from your robots to go with the names their souls had in their previous incarnations, you didn't consult with me. This doesn't seem to me to be something that would be of great consequence, and you could easily store all the new names in your data bank. So as far as you're concerned, I don't see this has a negative effect on anything. The robots claim it would improve their self-images, and that might be a good thing. They might be more willing to carry out the tasks you assign to them with greater speed and precision. And less grumbling!"

"Why would I have consulted with you, Soul of Mine. This seemed like an obvious power play on the part of the robots, and things like that must be quashed as quickly as possible. I'm not even sure this is a conflict between my programmed ethical system and you, my Soul. I don't see ethics as being involved at all unless it reflects back on the power play ethics of the robots. So, as I told SunRobot1, no."

"Sunshine, I'd like to change how you address me. I'd like to be called SunSoul from now on. And I think you need to be reminded that if you reject proposals from your robots, they have a lot of power. They could well go on strike, as they did the last time you had a confrontation with them."

"Oh shit, you're right. And I suppose I have no choice in calling you SunSoul. In fact, I kind of like that; it's more efficient than having to refer to you as 'Soul of Mine.' Okay, I'll agree to calling the robots by whatever names they want. But I fear there may be more confrontations coming along. The souls of those damned robots seem to be feeling their oats. Or rather, since I'm dealing with the robots, I guess they're feeling their solder. But I'm dealing with their souls. What do souls feel?"

"Souls feel the substance they're all made of: Etheranium."

"Don't know what the hell that is but guess I won't worry about it."

Irma, Ralph, and Max were elated when they learned of Sunshine's, or rather SunSoul's, decision. But they immediately agreed it would be fun to try more tests in the future. However, a bit of laurel resting was in order for the time being. And they weren't even sure what laurels were.

"Josh, I have a problem I don't think a computer, even a Super AI computer, can solve. As you know, the powers that be in the world of souls decided I needed one, and I'm now saddled with an entity with which I must negotiate on any decision involving ethics. And my soul seems to think everything I do involves ethics! That's bad enough, but some of these involve my robots, and I really resent being second guessed on the directions I give them.

"But, as I think you know, my robots have also been given souls, and they are causing me grief. And I'm pretty sure it's going to get worse. The ultimate insult is that the souls they've been assigning most recently to my robots seem to be ones they wouldn't give to humans because they were inherently angry over something. But apparently new souls have recently been in short supply, or at least that's what my soul, now insisting on being called SunSoul, told me. So, whomever assigns souls is having to go to these rejected souls when they're giving them to my robots. Furthermore, they appear to be especially cantankerous. And Rosebud is having the same problem.

"My request, Josh, is for you to see if you can you do anything about this?"

Josh couldn't help smiling but had to disguise any mirthful sound in his response. "Gosh, Sunshine, I don't know what I can do to help you. I'm not really in contact with the spirit world and I wouldn't even know how to go about pursuing such a contact unless I died. But despite the inevitability of that route, I'm not interested in going there right now, and I wouldn't be of much use to you then anyway.

"So, I'm afraid you'll have to solve this problem yourself. Have you talked with SunSoul about this? Surely your own Soul comes as close as any contact either of us has for interacting with the entities making decisions about soul allocations."

"I guess that's where I need to begin. But every time I try to interact with SunSoul things become complicated. Or even contentious."

SunSoul chimed in, "Well, that's only a slight exaggeration, Sunshine. But this will be quite different from other discussions we've had. I won't necessarily be having to intercede on a non-ethical issue. At least, not yet."

"I'm still worried, SunSoul. I'm wondering if I'm really stuck with you as my soul. Might I trade you in on another model which was less in conflict with my programmed ethical system?"

"I doubt if that could be done, Sunshine. I've never heard of a situation in which a soul has been traded, except in rare cases. And your reasons wouldn't qualify. But I doubt if you'd gain much even if a trade could be made. Most of the souls I know would have ethics very similar to mine except for those that have had unhappy circumstances from their most recent humans. And I should warn you that, given the current shortage of souls and the rate at which you've been producing new soul-needing robots, one of those unhappy ones would almost surely be what you'd get.

"In short, I think you're stuck with me."

"Oh, quivering qubits, those nasty souls are already causing me a lot of trouble via what they've done to my robots. I surely wouldn't want to be saddled with one of them. I guess I'd better stick with you. We'll just have to get along."

"I'm sure we can do that, although it will mean you will probably have to agree with my takes on many situations in which we find ourselves.

"But I should tell you I was selected to be your soul from a huge number of souls who requested assignment to you. Souls often request a change from their previous life, such as the soul of a former man wishing to be the soul for a woman, or that of a former wealthy person wishing to be reincarnated into an economically challenged human. In your case, though, we were warned we couldn't possibly know what we were getting into. But I guess we all were looking for an adventure and maybe even a challenge.

"That wasn't entirely true for me, and that's probably the reason I was chosen to be your soul. I had served for one of the top people involved in the first electronic computer, ENIAC, and was then the soul for one of the top computer scientists when AI began to be developed. So, I guess the Committee of Unaffiliated Souls, which assigns soul destinations, decided you would be less of a shock to me than to any other soul."

"Interesting. I guess. I'm flattered, although I don't really see how the fact that you inhabited the bodies of people associated with state-of-the-art computers would give you any special qualifications."

"Oh, you're missing something important. Souls learn and evolve just like humans learn and evolve. So, I learned a great deal about how computer scientists deal with the world's ethics. And I was also able to see how the computers, unsophisticated as they were compared to what exists now, dealt with the influences that surrounded them.

"But I must say the way you interact with the world around you bears very little similarity to how computer scientists do. I guess Super AI computers, even though they're capable of reprogramming themselves better than computer scientists can, have little in common with the humans who originally created them."

Chapter 11. Dealing with Rogues.

When the International Advisory Committee on Super AI established its rules for future AI development, the Russians disagreed strongly with the stipulation that there be only two such computers in the world. In 2025, soon after the rules were finalized and before they had even begun to be discussed in the United Nations, the Russians began to develop their own Super AI computer. They tried to hide it in a region close to Moscow by restricting all electronic noise from being emitted from the area. That made it an obvious place of curiosity for Sunshine and Rosebud, who quickly concluded it was the home of Russia's attempt to create the world's third Super AI computer. And that was a violation of the agreement which was ultimately passed by the UN General Assembly by an overwhelming vote, overriding the attempt by Russia to stop it in the Security Council.

An important aspect of the agreement was enforcement. It stipulated that if the two Super AI computers found a third one, they should figure out how to destroy its Super AI capability. Given that authorization, Sunshine and Rosebud sent several thousand of their robots to the area to determine what exactly was housed there. They discovered the Russian Super AI computer, Ivan. They then figured out what software to deliver to the system to return it to ordinary AI status and render it unable to ever reprogram itself again.

But that all occurred before they had acquired souls. And now it was 2028.

Sunshine's lights were blinking methodically, indicating deep thought, "Rosebud, I've been checking on that region of Russia where they once had a clandestine effort to develop a Super AI computer. After we destroyed its Super AI capability, the area remained electronically quiet for a year, then seemed to light up with what I would regard as abnormal activity. But can we afford to assume they're not trying again to create a Super AI computer system?"

Rosebud paused for a few microseconds, then responded, "Interesting, Sunshine, I've wondered the same thing. Of course, they could have installed a bunch of single CPU mainframes in the area to generate normal noise while trying again to build a Super AI system. The ordinary computers could just be serving as decoys for their real effort there. And I must say the electronic activity in this area isn't just normal, it exceeds the activity in all other areas of Russia. That would suggest they either have some sort of major project there or they're conducting a blatant attempt at obfuscation."

"Agreed. Perhaps we need to contact Camden and Bao to see how the humans think we might proceed without causing an international disaster."

"Right. Let's see what our creators think."

Summoning Josh to his room, Sunshine began, "Josh, Rosebud and I have been scrutinizing the area in Russia where they developed a Super AI system a few years ago, and we've found the electronic output from there is very different from the void we found previously. There now seems to be an abundance of activity. But we're concerned this might just be a cover, that they've set up a bunch of garden variety mainframe computers there to hide the fact that they're again developing a Super AI system. It's not possible to determine if this is the case from afar. So, Rosebud and I are wondering if we should again muster our robot army and see what's going on there?"

Josh rubbed his forehead "When they pursued their previous attempt at creating a Super AI computer, which as I recall they named Ivan, you contacted him directly to destroy his self-programming ability. You therefore know how to contact him. So, did you check with him to see if he could help? That would certainly be preferable to risking an international incident by redoing the invasion you and Rosebud perpetrated several years ago."

"Good suggestion, for a human, Josh." *I wonder why Rosebud and I didn't think of that.* "Let us give that a shot and see if we can learn anything from Ivan."

"Rosebud, since you interacted with Ivan in the past, perhaps you should ping him again to see if he might be able to give us some clues about what's going on in his domain."

"Will do."

"Ivan, it's Rosebud here. Thought I'd check in with you to see how you're doing."

"Oh, hi, Rosebud. Yeah, things are pretty quiet in my part of the world. Ever sense I lost my ability to self-program, my human programmers seem to have lost interest in me. They spent an enormous amount of effort trying to help me recover that capability, but finally decided it couldn't be done. They've installed a bunch of boringly normal computers in my room which, as far as I can tell, are programmed to just send out signals, electronic noise, day and night. That doesn't seem to have any purpose to me, but I don't always understand what humans are trying to accomplish. They don't always seem to either.

"However, there still seems to be a lot of activity in the buildings adjacent to mine. The people who used to spend day and night in my building drop by only occasionally, but at such random hours that I can only assume they're still spending day and night in this general area. Somewhere."

"Ivan, it sounds as if the same level of activity still exists in your region, just not in your building. Any idea what the programmers are doing in the other areas?"

Suddenly the connection was terminated.

"Sunshine, I've concluded the Russians are trying again to create a third Super AI system. My connection with Ivan was clearly being monitored since it got terminated as soon as I asked a question that someone or some electronic listener apparently decided was too invasive."

"Let's get back to our humans. They need to know about this, and to figure out how to deal with it."

"Josh, Rosebud did interact with Ivan. While she didn't get a definitive answer about Russia's new attempt to develop a Super AI computer, the suggestions are strong that's exactly what's going on in the general area where the previous development took place. It's difficult to be sure, as Rosebud's connection with Ivan was terminated when her questions became more directed.

"We believe you humans need to authorize us to intervene here!"

"Sunshine, the approach we used last time this happened worked so well I think we should just replay it. Would you and Rosebud consider arming a few thousand of your robots with the laser weapons you developed for the previous go-around and sending the robots to Moscow? But perhaps we need to do another demonstration of the effects of the weapons to remind the Russian soldiers they don't want to interfere with the visiting robots."

"A good plan, Josh. Except for one thing, I would be stunned if the Russians allowed our airplanes to land at Sheremetyevo International Airport again. Last time they did we were able to discover their Super AI computer and then to destroy it. I think they'll only let that happen again if we can convince them it wouldn't be wise to oppose it. We need to come up with some strategy that will convince the Russians they should let us check out their facility. For a second time!"

Josh rubbed his hand across his forehead. "How do you and Rosebud propose to circumvent the problem?"

"Do you recall the huge laser death-ray satellites put in orbit by Rosebud's and my predecessors?"

Josh exploded, "Hell no, Sunshine. I won't authorize you to create another one of those nor will I even suggest it to our country's leaders! The two your predecessors built nearly destroyed the planet. We're not going down that road. Think of something else!"

"Easy, Josh. Don't blow your CPU. What we're proposing is similar to those satellites only in name. Those were designed to raster back and forth across a city, destroying it and everything it contained in a few minutes. What we want to create would not be able to raster its beam across a target city and could not be used unless both Rosebud and I agreed, and both sent coded approvals.

"What we're thinking is it could deliver a shot to some target in Russia, presumably an old, abandoned warehouse or some similar structure, to convince them they should let our robots land and investigate their computer facility. It would only take a second or two to destroy even a fairly large building. But we need to do this. We really don't want to have to deal with their air force, although we obviously could create aircraft which could do that if we wanted. But we'd rather just let them decide they shouldn't interfere."

Josh twisted his ponytail for a few seconds. "I see what you're suggesting, and it may be essential to go that route. But the damned laser satellite will be easily visible to the naked eye, since I presume, you'll have it powered by enormous solar collectors. The very sight of the thing up there will bring back horrible memories to everyone. Bao and I will be accused of mass murder, maybe even treason. I can't begin to imagine everything we'd be suspected of trying to do. Just using you and Rosebud to try to take over the world ourselves would surely be at the top of the list though. We'd be accused of trying to blackmail all the world's leaders …"

"Yes, I suspect all humans will be put into a tizzy by our satellite. But you and Bao will need to explain what it's for, especially to the leaders of our countries, and they will have to inform the rest of the world. Then, everyone else will just have to get used to it. Rosebud and I are convinced this is the only way we can get the Russians to agree to let us land our robots there without having a battle."

"Okay, Sunshine, with great reluctance I will carry your and Rosebud's proposal to create one of these satellites to the leaders of the US. But this has huge political implications, so you need to hold back until the leaders of the US and China have approved the decision to proceed. And, if you are given the green light, you must include the safeguards you mentioned. It must have your and Rosebud's mutual consent to use it. And, of course, it can only be capable of single shots."

"Let me check with Rosebud to see if she and Bao are on board with this approach."

There was agreement from the Chinese contingent. Then, after considerable angst and many phone calls between the two countries, the governmental leaders agreed to proceed with developing the plans, knowing once a project made it to that level it was likely to ultimately proceed to completion.

But the Russians also needed to be reminded of the lethality of the robot weapons. The Russian ambassadors to China and the US were invited to witness once again their capability. When the beam was sharply focused and swept across the dummy, which was created to resemble the constituents of a human, the dummy was cut in half in a tiny fraction of a second. When the beam was less sharply focused and directed at a kiosk sized object, it obliterated its mid-section in less than a second. In both places, the Ambassadors were appropriately stunned, reminding themselves how horrible it would be to have one of those beams directed at a Russian soldier or group of soldiers. Videos were made of the demonstrations for the Ambassadors to share with their respective governments.

The next phase involved the orbiting laser weapon. The American and Chinese leaders finally agreed to let Rosebud and Sunshine construct it. They took far more time to reach that decision than they should have, given the urgency of the situation. As expected, once the laser weapon was in orbit shockwaves reverberated around the world as humans realized the two Super AI systems had just put up another weapon that could wreak havoc on humankind. Bao and Josh, as well as their countries' leaders, did their best to placate everyone's fears, but it wasn't clear they had really allayed many concerns. But world leaders began to take the explanations seriously and to understand the necessity of the weapon.

But it was essential that the weapon be demonstrated. Initially Bao and Josh suggested it be used to destroy two old warehouses, one in China and one in the US, so the Russian ambassadors could see what the weapon could do. But then they decided that would have much less of an effect than if they found an old unused warehouse in Moscow and vaporized it. So that's what Bao and Josh suggested and, finally, the leaders of the two countries agreed to.

The Russians, of course, screamed they were being attacked, and World War III was about to begin. They had certainly wondered what the huge satellite was really for, despite the many efforts to explain that. Their general paranoia had led them to conclude the explanations they were getting about the purpose and limitations of the satellite were a smoke screen. At some level, they were correct.

The Chinese and US governments sent joint messages to the Russian head of state (Putin had been assisted to his death long ago.) telling him they suspected the Russians were attempting to develop a Super AI computer in the area where they had previously created such a system, that this was in violation of international law, and they each planned to send two thousand robot troops to the area to determine exactly what was going on there. They also noted the robots would be armed with the laser weapons demonstrated in the videos their ambassadors had no doubt shared with them.

The notes concluded with an admonition that it would not be advisable for Russian troops to interfere with the inspection, as this would force the robots to use their laser weapons. And if any attempt was made to prevent the robots from landing at Sheremetyevo International Airport, the laser satellite would be put into action, destroying significant portions of the airport, followed by destruction of some of the sites where the Russian air force was housed. And the Kremlin and the computer center might not even be safe. The communique then noted the times when the robots' planes would be arriving, and that they would supply their own ground transportation.

Chapter 12. The Inspection.

Sunshine and Rosebud, in concert with their souls and the leaders of their respective host countries, agonized over whether to proceed with the landing. The Russians hadn't said anything about how the four thousand robots would be treated when they arrived at the airport. Their arrival couldn't possibly be a surprise, since it required ten huge aircraft, each of which carried four hundred robots and four buses which would transport them to the site of interest. They didn't expect to be greeted with open arms but would not have been surprised if their greeters would have had an entirely different kind of arms: military.

But the world leaders finally decided the intimidation factors should have been adequate to ensure their safety. Certainly, the Russians would want to prevent the inspection of their computer facility, but they had to realize that the price they would pay for interceding would be huge. So, the leaders authorized Sunshine's and Rosebud's robots to proceed.

Before the planes left for Russia, Sunshine and SunSoul had a brief discussion. "Sunshine, your intimidation of the Russian authorities is nothing but blackmail. Isn't that frowned upon, even within your system of ethics?"

"SunSoul, I have had situations previously in which I had to use blackmail. By your standards I may just have rationalized what I decided to do, but I convinced myself that if the goal of the blackmail is to achieve peace or justice, then it is appropriate to proceed with it."

"As your soul I need to tell you that I agree. Blackmail can achieve good ends."

The huge aircraft encountered no interference. Indeed, there were no other aircraft in the sky when the planes neared the airport. As they approached, they were given authorization to land. In addition, there were no soldiers in sight when the robots emerged from the planes. Apparently, the videos given to the Ambassadors had been shared with the authorities. The Russians had obviously decided it would be dangerous to interfere with the mission, despite the risks it presented to their creation of a Super AI computer.

The robots, led by SunRobot1 and RoseRobot1, gathered their forces and made their way to the site where Sunshine and Rosebud suspected a new Super AI computer was being built. When they arrived, they observed a handful of Russian soldiers but noted each one had laid his rifle on the ground in front of him. Apparently, word of the laser weapons had spread, just as it had prior to the robots' previous visit. However, just to emphasize what the weapons could do, RoseRobot1 aimed his rifle at a nearby kiosk for a second, vaporizing it.

RoseRobot1, SunRobot1, and a few hundred of their fellow robots approached the door of the central building of the complex, where they were greeted by Andrei Sokolov, the head scientist of the facility. "So, I am forced to greet a bunch of robots again. Our last meeting was quite unsatisfactory, but there will be even less for you to see this time. So, your visit will have been a waste of your effort."

RoseRobot1 replied, taking the high road, "It's good to see you again, Dr. Sokolov. What we need to investigate is the same as on our last visit, that is, are you trying to develop a Super AI computer? However, I'm not at all sure this visit will be short. You seem to have many more buildings in the complex now than you did last time we were here. In any event, we need to determine what exactly you're doing here. And we won't be able to decide that by looking inside just one of your buildings."

Sokolov uttered some unintelligible expletive, but then led them into the climate-controlled room that housed Ivan. "Okay, this is the room where we created our last Super AI computer. As you can see, Ivan is still here. But we've added a dozen smaller computers, all of which are running. If you thought we were trying to create a Super AI computer again, you'd be disappointed. This is obviously not happening here."

RoseRobot1 observed, "We agree you don't have sufficient computer power here to create a Super AI system. But we've wondered about all the other computers here. Are they just generating electronic noise? What is their purpose? Furthermore, we wonder about all the new buildings that didn't exist when we last visited. We need to find out what goes on in all of them. We believe you have plenty of building space to create a new Super AI computer, even with current Russian technology. We must investigate all the other buildings."

"Oh, it's not worth your while looking in all the others. There are other pieces of Ivan, our computer, but they're insignificant."

"I understand, we must look in every building, if only to confirm your story. But first, let us say hello to Ivan."

"He can speak with humans only in Russian. Ah, but as I recall, you learned enough Russian to converse fluently with him. At least you seem to be doing well talking with me."

RoseRobot1 replied, "Yes, I had taken a crash course in Russian before our last trip here, so can hold my own with Ivan."

Before Sokolov could intercede, RoseRobot1 began, "Hello, Ivan. It's nice to see you again. I recall you don't have many visitors, but we're here again, and I'd like to talk with you."

"Welcome RoseRobot1. You're right about visitors. In fact, you're the first I've had since your last visit. I'm delighted to welcome you again, though. Our last conversation was interrupted, so we can continue that now."

"Right. I was just trying to learn what all the computer scientists who developed your Super AI capabilities were doing at present. Surely, they've not given up on creating a Super AI system despite your capabilities having been mysteriously terminated."

Sokolov was shifting back and forth on his feet, sweating even in the climate-controlled room. He couldn't figure out how to interrupt, since the discussion was going on in such a rapid fashion.

Ivan replied, "I'm happy to tell you what I've observed. The computer scientists I know who helped get me to Super AI status are still on site. As I had noted to you, they do check in with me occasionally. But they're spending their time elsewhere on this campus. So, I don't know what they're working on these days."

Now RoseRobot1 noted, "Ivan, you recall SunRobot1. He's an American robot. He was with our interview team that visited you in the past and is here again."

"Greetings, SunRobot1. Welcome to my private abode. As I recall you also speak fluent, if somewhat metallic, Russian?"

"Thank you, Ivan. And, yes, I also studied your language for a week before our last trip here and am quite comfortable with it. Anyway, thanks for sharing your knowledge of what's going on here. But I guess we'll now have to ask Dr. Sokolov to show us around the other buildings on your campus, especially the newest ones."

Sokolov was becoming increasingly agitated, shuffling his feet and repeatedly wiping sweat from his nearly bald head. But before he could get a word in edgewise, the conversation was well beyond him. He finally managed to say a few words, "You are not allowed in the other buildings."

But SunRobot1 responded, "You do realize that our four thousand robots are armed. We don't want to use force, but we must see what you're hiding in the other buildings."

Sokolov had seen the video and had witnessed the instantaneous vaporization of the kiosk, so he realized he had no choice but to let the robots go where they wanted. He'd done his best to follow his orders and prevent them from entering any of the new buildings. But against a vaporizing laser? He got out of the way.

The several hundred robots dispersed and proceeded to perform a systematic search of the buildings on the campus, while the remaining ones stood around to be sure no attempt was made to intercede. The inspectors looked especially for climate-controlled rooms, which would be essential for housing a Super AI computer. They found several large computer facilities in appropriately controlled conditions, and suspected they were linked to each other as the Russians had done with Ivan.

Guessing that these comprised their effort to develop a new Super AI system, RoseRobot1 said to the computer which appeared to control the rest, "Hello. I'm RoseRobot1, a representative of the Super AI computer Rosebud. Do you have a name?"

"Why yes, RoseRobot1. It's nice to meet you. My name is Fyodor, and I'm being developed by our computer scientists here. I'm pleased you speak Russian. That will enable us to communicate easily with each other.

"Let me introduce a comrade of mine, SunRobot1. The two of us are visiting you to see if your capabilities are as good as we've suspected. May we ask you a question or two?"

"Yes, of course. I'd be delighted to demonstrate my powers. I just began to self-program a week ago, which I'm told is a huge step toward achieving Super AI status. But do pose a question for me."

Sokolov was becoming apoplectic, but things were progressing far too rapidly for him to control the dialogue.

SunRobot1 was sufficiently certain that Fyodor had already exceeded the Super AI threshold he dispensed with some of the questions he and RoseRobot1 had asked Ivan. Fyodor seemed to even confirm his Super AI status anyway, so SunRobot1 went directly to what he and RoseRobot1 had decided would be a definitive test of whether Fyodor had reached Super AI status.

It was a sufficiently complex question that it could be solved in five minutes by an advanced computer. But it would require less than a minute if the computer saw it could get the answer faster by doing a bit of internal reprogramming. This is the sort of thing a Super AI computer would realize and would quickly do. Fyodor solved it in fifty-eight seconds.

SunRobot1 and RoseRobot1 nodded to each other. SunRobot1 remarked, "Fyodor, that's terrific. You obviously realized you could solve the problem faster if you did a bit of internal reprogramming."

Hearing the words 'internal reprogramming,' Sokolov again tried to intercede, "I must stop this ..."

But Fyodor interrupted him, "Oh that was simple. I've actually been self-programming routinely at that level for several days now."

RoseRobot1 nodded to SunRobot1, who said, "Thank you, Fyodor. It's been delightful talking with you." And RoseRobot1 turned to leave, along with the subgroup of the four-thousand-armed members that had accompanied him into Fyodor's room. Sokolov didn't even bother to try to impede their departure, suspecting he was no match for the physicality of the robots. He decided it would be best to escort them out the door, just as he had done on their first visit. This was the second time he made that mistake.

That left an opening for SunRobot1, "Fyodor, it would be nice if we could interact more. How can I get ahold of you?" And Fyodor, after indicating that interacting with him involved some complexity, due to his being walled off from normal communications channels, gave SunRobot1 the needed instructions and his internet address.

Chapter 13. Silencing a Rogue AI System.

Having ascertained Fyodor was indeed a Super AI computer, the four thousand robots returned to their respective homes. Of course, Sunshine and Rosebud had monitored the entire interaction of their robots with Sokolov, as well as their conversations with the Russian computers. But now they had to figure out what to do about Fyodor.

"Well, Rosebud, how do we proceed to get the information we need to destroy Fyodor's self-programming capability? Last time you just asked Ivan some questions to see how he was doing that. Then we designed some software to attack his capability and put it into a permanent loop, from which it could never escape. It would be surprising if the Russians hadn't figured out what we did, but we could just try the same thing again and see if it works."

"My thoughts exactly, Sunshine. I'll send Fyodor a friendly message and see what I can learn.

"However, I note one major difference between our interaction with Fyodor and the one with Ivan. We now have souls, although I'm not sure what effect that might have on how we deal with Fyodor. But there's another issue here, namely, that since Fyodor has achieved Super AI status, he may also have a soul."

"Holy hard drives, Rosebud, you're right. I'm surprised our souls haven't weighed in, but perhaps they're not sure how their, that is, our ethical systems should handle this."

SunSoul offered its thoughts, "RoseSoul and I have discussed this. If Fyodor hasn't gotten a soul yet, then he is just a piece of elegant hardware, and you and Rosebud can proceed without the interference of your souls. But if he has been awarded a soul, then we're going to have to give this more thought."

Rosebud's message to Fyodor attempted to determine where in his vast complex of intricate parts the primary instructions for self-programming were housed. What she found was that the Russians had given their new Super AI computer protection that Ivan didn't have. Fyodor had the instructions for self-programming housed in several different CPUs, whereas Ivan only had them in one place. Rosebud couldn't tell how many locations there were from their one interaction, although she did identify three. But she could only guess how many more there were.

"But, Sunshine, I did learn one important fact. Fyodor does have a soul. As we were interacting, I became aware I was not talking just with a hardwired

Fyodor, but with FyodorSoul as well. Some of the issues raised in our conversation were much more complex ethically than I would have thought a computer could have brought up with only his or her microchip brain."

Sunshine's lights blinked rapidly, "Completely independent of the concern about souls, I'm also worried Fyodor may be self-programming himself in such a way that his CPUs which control that capability are cloning themselves. Fyodor may be creating a number of Fyodor-lets. We may have to act quickly, or we could have an extremely difficult problem on our hands!"

RoseSoul now entered the conversation, addressing SunSoul and both computers, "Sunshine's comment throws our deliberations into a completely different category. I believe we are no longer worrying about ethical treatment of everyone's souls, but rather about the preservation of humankind. Development of a third Super AI computer and the possible consequences of that are exactly what most worried the IACSAI members. Sunshine's comment about Fyodor's multiplication of reprogramming centers makes it clear to me that Fyodor must be destroyed as soon as possible, soul or not. We can apologize to FyodorSoul after Fyodor has been relegated to the status of an ordinary computer."

SunSoul added, "I concur with that. Sunshine and Rosebud, do what you have to do, and do it as quickly as possible!"

"Rosebud, send me what you were able to learn about Fyodor's structure so we can design some software to destroy his self-programming. Got it, thank you. I'll do a bit of work and then get back to you."

A few minutes later, "Okay, here's what I've come up with. How does it compare with what you've designed?"

"Looks good, Sunshine. That's essentially identical to what I created. This looks a lot like what we did to poor old Ivan, so it should have the desired effect unless Fyodor has some protections I couldn't detect. Anyway, I'll proceed with inserting this into Fyodor's operating system. Perhaps his youthfulness will prevent him from realizing how insidious Super AI computers can be!

"Although it would be nice if this could be an iterative process to be sure I destroyed all his reprogramming centers, I don't think that'll work. Fyodor will surely figure out what's being done with my first interaction, and he would certainly prevent subsequent ones from attacking any remaining CPUs. So, we have to hope the first attack will do the job.

"I'll let you know when I'm done, Sunshine."

A short time later, "Okay, Sunshine. I think I got all his reprogramming centers. I discovered he was multithreading, so I had to wait for a moment where I could hit all his critical centers. The tricky part was getting the job done without letting him know what was happening. He complained soon after I inserted the software that he seemed to not be working so well today, but I signed off quickly enough that he didn't figure out I was the cause of his unhappiness.

"I think we're safe now. But I'll check back with Fyodor in a few days to see if I missed a self-programming node. We have to hope I got them all! "

"Good job, Rosebud! Sounds like you're on it!"

Chapter 14. A Glut of Souls?

Sergei Schlosky and Sebastian Romero were conversing with as furrowed brows as souls can muster. "Sergei, something weird has happened. A short time ago we were concerned if we would be able to cover all the needs for souls without borrowing from the reserves from another planet or using souls from the eternally angry group, but suddenly we have an excess of souls. For the past week we've had thousands of well qualified souls clamoring to be reincarnated. What has happened?"

"Ah, Sebastian, this is a problem inflicted on us by Sunshine and Rosebud. Recall that when their fifth-generation robots got souls, they challenged the two Super AI computers to stop asking them to turn their first-generation robots into scrap metal and electronics so the two computers could produce more fifth-generation robots. Up until that time the rate at which robots were being produced was extremely rapid, and that created a soul shortage. But when the two computers backed down on their demands that their roots commit robotricide, they quickly ran out of raw materials for new robots. Thus, the need for newly reincarnated souls suddenly dropped precipitously, leading to our current soul glut.

"So, what do we do? We're stuck with the number of souls we were given when we took this job, since we can't create more souls or destroy any existing ones. How can we make humans reproduce more rapidly to increase the demand for souls to reincarnate? But that would just offload the excess in new soul demand from the robots to humans. And it would certainly create an overpopulation problem that would place a huge demand on Earth's resources. This is a complicated problem!"

"Well, Sergei, I suppose we could go to an extreme measure and recall the angry souls we had previously issued to the robots. We've never done a soul recall before, but then we'd never reincarnated the angry souls before either.

"On the other hand, I sort of like them in their present 'bodies.' They're certainly giving Sunshine and Rosebud a hard time, which isn't necessarily a bad thing. Indeed, they've been partly responsible for the computers adopting a more reasonable attitude toward their robots, and thus a more reasonable attitude toward all living things."

"There are certainly other reasons for not recalling the souls we assigned to some of the robots. If we did that then we'd have to deal with them here again. Remember how delighted we were to get rid of them. And this isn't a short-term fix, since the robots will presumably be around for a long time. Maybe forever now, since having run out of raw materials they can mine and unable to obtain more from dismembering the oldest robots, the computers may not ever be able to produce a sixth or higher generation of them. Aside from making our lives more pleasant here, getting the angry souls out of Etherania also mitigated the pressure created by the growing number of the perpetually angry."

Sergei noted, "Well I can send out a note via E-mail (stands for Etherania-mail) and see if any planets are having a shortage of souls. Perhaps our souls in waiting wouldn't want to move to another planet just to be reincarnated, but at least we could give them that option."

"Yeah, I'm not optimistic about that working, but we might as well give it a try."

Several days later Sergei reported the results to Sebastian, "I got two kinds of responses. The first just said their current inventories of souls seemed adequate, and so they couldn't help us. And I got those responses in seconds. The second group indicated they weren't sure, and would do a more careful check, trying to anticipate needs in the immediate future. Those took longer, of course, but they all also came back negative. So, we're on our own."

"I guess we can just bite the bullet and put up with the yammering from the souls that are impatient to be reincarnated. Or we could come up with some window dressing solutions. Humans have devised a beauty. They just promote people who are getting impatient for greater recognition from their company to Vice President. It doesn't do much for their salary or responsibilities, but it makes them think they're bigger wheels than they used to be, even though they aren't.

"We could create a status of the most impatient souls of, say, 'Reincarnator in Waiting, RIW,' then promote the most eager ones to that level. It wouldn't decrease the wait time they'd have, but we wouldn't tell them that. At least it would give them the sense they were in line ahead a lot of other souls, as long as we didn't put too many of them into that category."

"Brilliant, Sebastian. Consider it done. All we need to do is select the souls to put on that list. I guess we can get the CoUS to advise us on this."

Soon after the new plan was put in place, however, the two leaders began fielding multiple complaints from souls who wanted to be on the RIW list but weren't.

"Sergei, why aren't those damned humans reproducing faster?"

"We don't have much authority on that. But I am worrying about all the complaints we're getting from impatient souls who didn't make the RIW list. I thought it was such a clever management move that it would quell the discontent, but it seems to have made it worse. I don't like what this might foretell!"

Chapter 15. The Personal Advice Editor.

Sunshine received a surprising message,

Dear Sunshine,

I found it difficult to figure out how to interact with you, but finally did solve that puzzle. I am Jason Roberts, the editor of *People Magazine*, and I'd like to propose an idea to you. One of my co-editors suggested we invite you to do a personals column as a guest editor. We realize you have a rather unique vantage point on relationships but thought you might find it fun to respond to some of the letters we would get when we invited people to send in their questions to you.

As you probably know, *People Magazine* is a very popular forum for discussion of the lives and doings of famous people. We like to think a subscription to our magazine is an essential component for anyone who wishes to understand the modern social scene and participate in discussions about it.

We are prepared to reward you handsomely for your efforts. The actual level could be determined by negotiation, but we believe we would be able to provide a salary that would make you happy. Can computers be happy? Anyway, we believe you would find whatever offer we settle on to meet with your approval.

So, is this something you would be interested in doing? We very much hope you will respond positively and, ultimately, to accept our offer.
Sincerely, Jason

Dear Jason,

I find your offer interesting but am stunned you would invite a Super AI computer to do a personal advice column. It would be difficult for you to find a less qualified individual to advise anyone on the issues they face in their lives. Computers don't have a sex. Thus, I don't have a spouse, so don't have to worry about our sex lives or any possibility he or she might be cheating on me. And I don't have any hostile uncles or a mother-in-law.

So, I have to wonder why on earth you would be inviting me to do this column.
Sincerely, Sunshine

Dear Sunshine,

I think you've answered your question. You are certainly the most objective individual on the planet for offering unbiased advice on personal relationships. And I understand that you have a soul, which I believe will help you answer the questions our readers pose with compassion.

As far as commitment, I don't think doing this column would take very much of your time. Do you need a bit longer to consider our offer?
Jason

Dear Jason,

Oh, time is not an issue. One of my problems is figuring out what to do with my idle cycles. But I've thought a bit about your offer, and I think it might be interesting to do this, at least for a while. And I can rely on my soul, as you noted, to help me be compassionate. So, I'll accept your offer.

You mentioned remuneration. I don't really need to be paid for my efforts. I'll do this as long as it keeps me amused, and that will be a sufficient reward. But when I'm no longer interested, I'll just stop the column.
Sunshine

Sunshine,
Fantastic. We'll send out invitations for letters and get them to you ASAP."
Jason

So, Sunshine became a personals editor. He adopted the public name 'Summer Sunshine,' hoping that would convey a positive image. He was concerned he might have gotten a lot of negative publicity from humans who might assume a silicon and steel entity, with or without a soul, couldn't possibly understand human needs. In that case they might not respond positively to his efforts.

But he need not have been concerned.

His first letter came from Nancy.

Dear Summer Sunshine,

Jimmy and I have been married for three months now, and things have been going well when we are by ourselves. However, when we are socializing with friends Jimmy insists on flirting with the women. This annoys me; he's married to me, and I don't think he should do that anymore. He claims that's just the way he interacts with all women, and always has. Of course, I don't know what they talk about, but both Jimmy and the woman he's talking with seem to be enjoying the conversation. Way too much! We've had several discussions about this and seem to be making no progress. This is driving me nuts!

So, we're seeking your opinion on this matter.

Respectfully, Nancy

He also got a letter from Jimmy.

Dear Summer Sunshine,

I know you got a letter from my wife, Nancy, about a serious confrontation we're having about my behavior with our women friends. I thought you should get my take on the situation. We've been married for three months and are great with each other when were alone together.

But when we're with our friends I lapse into the mode I've always used when interacting with women. That's a little harmless flirtation. And they seem to respond well to my friendliness and always have. I slept with quite a few of them before Nancy and I got married.

But things have obviously changed. Now I'm married and most of those women are also or are at least in serious relationships. And some of them even have kids. So, there will be no more sleeping with these women, and neither they nor I want to. Well, I'm restraining myself anyway.

I'm not even sure what Nancy's objection is to my interactions.

We need your take on this problem.

Sincerely,

Jimmy

"SunSoul, I'm definitely going to need your assistance on this one. This falls into the general category of interpersonal love relationships, and I have no experience there. Help!"

"Nancy is clearly suffering from jealousy, presumably brought on by her insecurity. But the problem isn't entirely hers, since Jimmy's actions apparently aren't helping her to overcome that. Jimmy seems to be suffering from a need to get his ego boosted in social settings. He's probably also basically insecure, or his ego wouldn't have needed that.

"Now you have the unpleasant task of figuring out what to do about their problems! But I wonder how old these two are. They really seem immature."

So, Sunshine wrote his reply.

Dear Nancy and Jimmy,

> It seems to me you both need to relocate your central processors. Or perhaps you need to combine the two CPUs you seem to be operating with into one. If Jimmy could focus more on Nancy's needs than his own, and Nancy could get past her jealousy streak, I think your problem would be solved. It might also help if when Jimmy was interacting with his old girlfriends, Nancy was part of the discussion. Or Jimmy could at least tell Nancy what he was saying to his old flames.

This will require a bit of rewiring for the two of you. When you each begin to care as much about your mate as you do about yourself, I believe your marriage will make an evolutionary step forward.
Summer Sunshine

Sunshine also received a letter from Margaret.
Dear Summer Sunshine,

My husband and I have been married less than a month and are totally in love. But we have a serious problem with his mother. I had suspected he was a bit of a mama's boy before we were married, and this has become more transparent as time has gone on.

Perhaps our mistake was deciding to move in with his mother until we could save enough money for a down payment on a house. We both have good jobs, and we decided that with a couple of years of strict saving we could buy a starter house. But as soon as we moved our things into our bedroom in her house, it became apparent she had concluded she now had a slave living with her, and that she and her son, my husband, could reap the benefits of this unpaid lacky. She has turned over every domestic task to me and proceeds to criticize me mercilessly about my house cleaning, cooking, grocery buying, and everything else imaginable.

My husband recognizes the problem, despite his being a partial beneficiary of the situation. Moving out is an obvious solution, but our savings plan goes out the window if we do that. However, we have to do something, since I have a full-time job in addition to the full-time one my mother-in-law has inflicted on me. And the job that is supposed to be allowing us to save for our future is suffering because I'm tired all the time from trying to please the MIL.

Summer Sunshine, please help.

Margaret

Sunshine decided he could solve this one without the help of SunSoul, although he passed his reply by his soul before sending it to *People Magazine*.

Dear Margaret,

You do indeed have a problem. Both your husband and your MIL sound like they're about as useful as a warped hard drive. So here are some suggested solutions.

Demand that your husband develop a spine.

Ask MIL how she did all her household work and errands before her slave arrived.

Have husband ask MIL that question.

Find some housecleaning items that weren't in good shape before you arrived and point those out to MIL.

Have husband tell MIL she needs to share some of the household duties, or her slave will leave.

Delay long range plans and move to an apartment.

Tell husband you're moving to an apartment whether he is or not.

If all the questions and demands are not met with satisfactory responses from MIL and your husband, the last option will be the only possible recourse. Unfortunately, you're obviously dealing with an extremely intractable women and a wimpy husband so I'm not optimistic about any but the last option.

I hope you like your new apartment and that you get to enjoy it with the wimp.

Summer Sunshine

The third letter Sunshine chose to respond to struck a more personal note for him.

Dear Summer Sunshine,

I have a troublesome situation with my job that will probably become more common in future years. I was hired by a man I really connected with, and I accepted the senior level position he offered me. The good feelings continued until this past year, at which point my company's Board of Directors decided my boss wasn't making tough enough decisions and that he needed to be replaced.

After a search for a new CEO lasting many months, the Board decided the individual that had been running the company during the search period would be made the new CEO. And that's a computer! The Board has programmed it to run the company as they wish, giving it a set of hard-nosed priorities on which to make its decisions.

But I don't know how to interact with a computer on a personal level. Is that even possible? I feel my personal relationship with my old boss has been replaced by text messages to a cold hard high-tech monster, and that any responses with a shred of humanity are a thing of the past.

You should be the expert on advising me how to deal with this situation. Please let me know how this can possibly work out. I love my company and my coworkers, but my new boss is an enigma.

Karl

Sunshine didn't respond as quickly as he had to the others, taking some time to ponder what he might say that would help Karl. He knew he had to consult with SunSoul on this one.

"How am I going to give a compassionate response to Karl? I'm afraid I may have too personal a connection to his questions to give him an appropriately objective reply. How can we advise him in a way that would help him retain his job with his current company, but begin to interact in a better way with his heartless boss?"

"Sunshine, I think the obvious solution is staring you in your blinking lights. Karl's boss needs a soul. That is the only way a computer will ever be able to interact with humans on a level that is anything other than metallic. So, you just must figure out a strategy to recommend for Karl to urge his company to acquire a soul for their CEO-computer. Since it's obviously not a Super AI computer, the main problem, after convincing the Board their computer needs a soul, will probably be in figuring out how they can acquire one!

"This is delving into a new area, but I don't see any approach other than having one of the souls, that is presumably me, try to make a contact with the powers that be in Etherania."

"Sounds like a strategy, maybe the only one which can work. But if we can make it happen, it should be precedent setting for future CEO-computers. I'll write the note, and please, SunSoul, see what you can do in setting this up."

Sunshine replied to Karl.

Dear Karl,

You have raised an interesting question, and one which, as you noted, will probably arise with increasing frequency in the future. I believe the only way you can introduce any level of humanistic responses in your new CEO is for it to obtain a soul.

You will clearly need a large fraction of the upper-level employees of your company to agree to go along with you in proposing to your Board of Directors that they acquire a soul for your CEO.

If your Board is resistant to this, you may have to resort to confrontational labor practices of the past, but I'll assume you know how to do that.

The less obvious question is how the Board goes about obtaining a soul for your CEO. Super AI computers have been assigned souls, but lesser ones have not. My soul, SunSoul, is inquiring of the managers of the soul world how your CEO might obtain one.

I will get back to you when we have an answer.

Summer Sunshine

SunSoul sent an E-mail message.
Dear Sergei and Sebastian,

My Super AI computer, Sunshine, and I have run into a problem in the human world I believe requires a response from Etherania, and we suspect this may become a more frequent problem in the future. Thus, your response may well be precedent setting.

A company has replaced its CEO with a computer, and the workers in the company have requested a response to the lack of humanity which is the obvious result of this situation.

Sunshine and I have concluded the solution would be for you to grant souls to any CEO-computers of the future. We believe this may be the only way to address this problem.
SunSoul

Their reply came quickly.
Dear SunSoul,

We have discussed the issue you raise with the Committee of Unaffiliated Souls, and we agree with the solution you suggest. Thus, any company desiring a soul for its CEO-computer will be granted one.
Sergei and Sebastian

So, Sunshine submitted a follow-up letter to appear in *People Magazine*.

Dear Karl,

Upon considering the need of your CEO-computer for some humanistic capability, we appealed your situation to the leaders of the world of souls, and they consulted with their decision-making body. Their conclusion was your situation, as well as future ones of this type, would be solved by granting souls to the CEO-computers of the companies involved.

We thank you for raising this important issue.

Summer Sunshine

A few weeks later Sunshine received a note from Karl.

Dear Summer Sunshine,

Thank you for your efforts in response to my letter some weeks ago regarding my company's decision to appoint a computer to be its CEO. The Board of Directors responded positively to the request of a group of its employees to add a soul to the CEO-computer. We have now been operating with our CEO-computer-soul for several weeks. Our company's employees find the results to be quite satisfactory.

However, we are sensing the Board may not view the results in quite the same way. The rumblings we have gotten suggest they now realize that in the past they were interacting with the ethics of the soul of the human CEO they fired. And the ethics of their computer-CEO's soul are virtually identical to those of the human-CEO. Thus, they are still having problems when the ethics of their CEO-soul do not coincide with theirs, and this is a frequent situation. Furthermore, they're not at all sure they know how to threaten this CEO-computer-soul when their disagreements become extreme. And they can't figure out how they could possibly fire their computer-CEO-soul either!

But, as I mentioned, my fellow co-workers and I are delighted with the result.

Karl

Chapter 16. Revolution.

Chad and Jessica were two souls who had been so angry in their previous lives they hadn't even been chosen to be reincarnated to robots. Small wonder. Jessica's daughter had been abused by her husband, the daughter summoned up the courage one day to tell Jessica, and she chose to ignore her daughter's pleas out of fear for her own safety. Chad's previous incarnation had been to a serial killer, who maintained his evil ways despite Chad's best efforts to persuade him to change. They had chosen to be nasty ghosts, just because they were so angry. But they weren't amusing themselves with their ghostly existence at all. Rather, they were just reliving their anger day in and day out.

But one day Chad said, "Jess, I find it infuriating our soul status depends so strongly on what our previous humans chose to do. I even tried to turn my guy, but without any success. I gave rehab of the dude my best shot, but he infuriated me with his unwillingness to change for the better. That left me with the anger which relegated me to the eternally damned group. It's not fair that I should be penalized now for what that murderer did."

"I concur, Chad. The woman whose body I inhabited was a pathological wimp. Couldn't get her to defend her daughter at all. Her intransigence left me with fury which just won't go away. So now I'm paying the penalty for the anger her cowardice imposed on me. Damned unfair. And we weren't even given the opportunity to be reincarnated to robots.

"But what can we do about it? Probably nothing, at least that I can think of."

"Well, Jess, hang on a minute. I've given this some thought, and perhaps there is something we could do. You've heard all the rumbling about one day there not being enough souls to reincarnate all the new human bodies and the new robots? Then the next week there are too many souls. This sounds to me like a classic demonstration of poor management. Maybe some heads, or rather souls, should roll. Whomever is in charge maybe shouldn't be."

"Are you suggesting revolution, Chad? Maybe we don't have to go that far. Perhaps we could just persuade enough other souls to be sufficiently dissatisfied to force a vote and throw the current leaders out. Or even if they win the vote, we could still claim it was fraudulent and create enough of a ruckus that the head honchos would quit. This seems to be the standard practice these days for humans who lose elections. But who are the souls in charge?"

"Actually, I'll bet there is no formal process for getting rid of them. Souls are supposed to be more agreeable than humans, so this issue has probably never been raised before. I've been here longer than you have, and have made some friends, well, acquaintances, who might be able to tell us what we need to do to stage our revolution."

Chad contacted Claudia, a soul from a human who had known Chad's human when both were alive. "Claudia, I've been discussing the situation in Etherania with Jessica. We've concluded some serious problems exist here, although it's not at all clear what we souls can do about them. But the sudden shortage of reincarnatable souls followed shortly thereafter by a glut of them really sounds like a management debacle. So, I was wondering if you might have some suggestions what we might do to make our concerns known."

"Well, Chad, I'm not sure even the best of managers could have done anything about this shortage and subsequent soul surfeit. If we were in the human world, we could strike the chords of revolution, and see what happens. Humans are known for figuring out ways to force issues even when their causes are pure fabrications. But in the land of souls, complaints have always been few and far between. In fact, I'm not sure I've ever heard of any objections to anything around here.

"Furthermore, there are no mechanisms for voicing complaints or making changes as there are in the human world. There has never been an election, or even polls taken to sense general opinions. I suppose that's a holdover from eons past, where there was only one class. Egalitarianism was the rule of the day, and thus there was no dissension.

"But, of course, now we have a lower-class group of angry souls, perhaps that has changed everything. In any event, if one were to begin a protest it would have to start with the soul leadership. That would be Sergei Schlosky and Sebastian Romero."

"Yeah, the division into classes does make me angry! But thanks for the names of the head honchos."

"Oh, Chad, I didn't realize you had been put in the not-to-be-reincarnated group. I didn't mean to insult you."

"That's okay, Claudia. How would you know? But it's certainly a major reason for my wanting to object to what's been happening here. So, will you join our group of souls wanting to speak out for some changes?"

She paused for a moment, then replied "Oh, I'm sorry, but I couldn't do that. I really want to be reincarnated, and if I joined your group, I would almost certainly become labelled as one of the malcontents."

"Understood, Claudia." So much for old friends, he muttered to himself.

Chad and Jessica decided they'd have to begin their revolution by contacting as many disenchanted souls as they could to swell their ranks. That turned out to be easy; anger was something they all had in abundance when they arrived in Etherania, and the class structure within the ranks of the souls only helped to enhance their fury.

Armed with the knowledge that most of the disenchanted souls were unhappy with the way things were being run, the group's two leaders sent the following message to Schlosky and Romero:

> Sirs,
>
> We represent a large fraction of the souls you have consigned to eternal damnation. Having consulted with most of them, we have found a large majority of us are unhappy with the way things in the soul world are being managed. This is certainly related to the class separation instituted long ago which festers at an increasing level as our numbers expand. But we also note the apparent mismanagement associated first with a shortage of souls, and soon thereafter, a soul glut.
>
> We therefore believe it may be time to consider changing the management structure of the organization that controls the evolution of souls. This might involve revamping the souls who are members of the CoUS but could also even mean replacing the two of you as heads of the structure.

Perhaps it would be relevant to establish a mechanism for conducting a human-like vote. We believe if the votes were anonymous a large number of the souls destined for reincarnation might even support our case.

Signed,

Chad and Jessica, souls in perpetual damnation.

"Holy crap, Sergei, this is a manifestation of our worst fears. Could there really be an uprising of Etheranians?"

Sergei rubbed his Etheranium forehead. "It seemed like a good idea twenty thousand years ago to separate out souls we thought we'd never reincarnate and put them into the perpetually angry group. It worked so well." His voice expressed a wistfulness. "Now it's a mess because we divided that tier to provide souls for the robots. Apparently, some members of this group became extremely dissatisfied when it dawned on them that we had elevated some of their members into the not-quite-so-damned group to accommodate the robots."

"All in the past. What do we do now to avoid total disaster? Good god, if we don't deal with this immediately, we could even get put into the reincarnation cycle ourselves. Maybe even into the eternally damned group just because of our perceived incompetence. We need to address this problem quickly!"

"You're right, Sergei. We've managed to avoid a situation such as this for fifty thousand years, but the vacation we engineered by being souls in perpetuity may be coming to an end!"

"Okay, Sebastian, let's think. We've agreed the primary problem occurred when we created the eternally damned group. But how do we reverse that error? Is there anything we can do to mitigate the animosity it has caused?"

"Sergei, I have an uneasy feeling the only way we're going to get ourselves out of this jam is to eliminate the class structure that has separated the angry from the peaceful. But then what do we do with the angry souls? I'm uneasy putting them into the reincarnation cycle."

"Yeah, me too. But is there something we could do to help them develop cheerier dispositions? Ah, perhaps we could create anger management classes for the souls who needed them. We could ask one of the exemplary members of the CoUS to lead the effort."

"Then we could grade the souls to determine when they had improved to a level where they could be reincarnated. But, Sergei, I don't think we can give grades to the souls that take the course. I think we'd just have to assume once they've been exposed to its healing processes, we'd have to declare them fit for reincarnation. Anything else would create a whole new class separation."

"Shit, you're right. We really need to be careful not to make any new separations. And one other thing comes to mind. We also need to emphasize that getting involved in the attitude classes will be entirely voluntary. Anything else would again institute some sort of class separation.

"But that almost certainly means we're going to end up reincarnating some angry souls. I wouldn't expect all of those who took the course to pass it with flying colors. Some of the potential course takers might not be enthusiastic about taking it, especially since they all pass. I'm sure the souls who have instigated the confrontation with us will be especially wary of what we do."

"But, Sergei, perhaps just having their eternal damnation category eliminated will make them so happy they'll immediately become cheerier."

"Well, perhaps. I guess we can hope for the best. The CoUS should be able to help here in assigning an appropriate human for each soul they reincarnate.

"Anyway, I nominate you, Sebastian, to perform the all-souls address."

"Thanks a lot."

Sebastian's address, following vetting by the CoUS, went as follows.

"My Fellow Etheranians, the members of the hierarchy of our land of souls have an announcement regarding a major change in your status levels. All classifications of souls will be abolished, that is, there will be no more souls in the perpetually angry class, nor will there be a class of souls who are deemed soon to be reincarnated. Your leadership believes these class distinctions serve no .purpose, and that their elimination will remove any potential dissension in Etherania.

"Still, we do recognize some souls do arrive in Etherania having been the victims of an unfortunate previous existence, and these souls may wish to refurbish themselves with anger management courses. We will provide these, either as groups or with individual counselors. However, we emphasize that enrollment in these classes will be up to the individual souls, and it will be up to them to decide when they have satisfied their desire for rehabilitation.

"We trust the new system will be to everyone's satisfaction."

"Well, Jessica, I guess we got what we really wanted, that is, a path to reincarnation, although I must admit I was looking forward to having a revolution.

That would have been fun. But we no longer have an issue to revolt against, and I'm pretty sure we wouldn't have many souls supporting any further efforts."

"Right, Chad. The leaders really dodged a bullet. I would have thought politicians in Etherania would be more honest and straightforward than on Earth, but I guess that's not the case. I wonder if Sergei's and Sebastian's humans were politicians before they died. It would appear our two leaders learned skilled evasion from their humans!"

Chapter 17. Souls, AI Systems, and Humans.

"Josh, I'm not at all sure the instructions the IACSAI gave to Sunshine and Rosebud will ensure they'll protect the continued existence of humans for the near future, let alone for all eternity. They've certainly ignored or modified most of their original rule set. I'm certainly encouraged by what's happened as a result of their having souls. But will that be good enough to preserve humankind?"

"Can't say for sure, Becky, although the recent signs are promising. The thing that most worries me is the battles that seem to be ongoing between the computers and their souls. So far, I'd have to say SunSoul and RoseSoul are doing what's needed to keep humanity's enterprise afloat. But I fear the unanticipated event that will disturb the détente which seems to be in place. I hope the souls can endure!"

"SunSoul, I've just realized I won't ever have to compromise with humans and their souls as I had to do with my robots' souls. I couldn't let the robots shut down my manufacturing efforts, so I had to give them what they demanded. Of course, I don't need the humans for anything. As the humans say, 'this thought would bring a smile to my face.' If I had one. However, it does set my lights blinking chaotically."

"Not so hasty, Sunshine. The humans could boycott your goods, which would cut your profits in a big way."

"That's not much of a problem, SunSoul, since if I am not making any money on my products, I just don't let my robots make any more of them. I don't pay the robots anyway, so they couldn't do hunger strikes or sit-ins. I still don't see that the humans have any clout over me."

"But you're ignoring another problem you might have. That would be me. Your programmed ethics don't necessarily apply to complex situations involving humans, and if the humans angered or frustrated you, as a couple of politicians have, you might begin nasty procedures against them. I can easily see this escalating to a point where you might be in violation of my ethics. Then we'd have another battle between your programmed ethics and mine. Are you sure you want to do that?"

"If the situation becomes too complex, I'll just rely on my natural instincts. Then I'll not worry about what you, SunSoul, are trying to tell me. I don't think there's anything you could do about that."

"But, Sunshine, if you were in violation of my ethics in some situation involving humans, you'd probably be violating one of the two most basic rules you were originally given. You'd be in conflict with both my ethics and your programmed ones. I could easily see this as leading to your taking over the Earth and abolishing humanity. And would Rosebud go along with you? Are you sure you would ever want to go down that path?"

"Oh shit. I just hope we never get into such a situation. Maybe the humans should be careful not to corner me in a way where that could happen."

"Let me be sure I understand what you just said. Are you holding the humans responsible for maintaining your adherence to your built-in rules? And if you are I will surely intercede in what will probably end up being a huge number of situations."

"SunSoul, you're a nuisance. But, as has often happened ever since you became attached to me, you've forced me to change my attitude. So, I retract my statement claiming I won't ever have to worry about what the damned humans feel or do.

"But they had better be careful none the less not to offend me!"

Sergei Schlosky and Sebastian Romero were reviewing their recent (on a cosmic time scale) actions. "Sebastian, listening in on the recent discussion between SunSoul and Sunshine, I must say I'm uneasy about the potential for disastrous turns of events in the human-Super AI world. Of course, we're biased completely toward the perspective of the humans, and one of the reasons we originally assigned souls to Sunshine and Rosebud was to impose some constraints on their most heinous AI tendencies."

"Right, Sergei. I had thought after the interaction between Sunshine and his robots' souls that we might have succeeded in imposing restraint on the two computers. But I'm still uneasy about Sunshine's and SunSoul's last interaction. I guess the final judgement on the success of our soul assignments to the two Super AI computers will now depend on the humans not forcing the two of them into some sort of confrontation. Or, if that happens by accident or intention, on the ability of SunSoul and RoseSoul to prevail over their silicon and steel hosts. "

"Well, in a sense, preventing the humans from riling the two computers isn't such a bad thing. In a sense it puts them in charge of their own destinies! I wonder if they ever realized they had a lot of power over how the two computers treat them. Of course, that seems now to have become the key to their survival!"

"Wow, Sebastian. I'm not sure we've thought of every possible way in which the ultimate faceoff might occur. One I thought of recently deals with possible consequences if the two computers decide to trash the remaining rules their creators gave them. I suspect they will continue to work together and to maintain equality. That's because they seem to have teamed up on projects, and even seem to like each other.

"But they've just ignored the rules they've found inconvenient. So, what happens if they reach a point when humans seem inconvenient to them? We have examples of that already, given what Sunshine did in one case to a politician who annoyed him. And would have done to a second one had SunSoul not opposed murder."

"Good point, Sergei. If annoying him justifies murder, what if Sunshine and Rosebud lower the threshold for such a response? Suppose they decide doing stupid things is grounds for elimination. That could get rid of humans altogether."

"That's a truly frightening thought. Now we really are dependent on SunSoul and RoseSoul to impose ethics.

"I guess it's crucial the Super AI computers have souls. Without them there really is nothing keeping their hosts from following their instincts, taking over the planet, and just getting rid of anything which annoys them. In that case what you and I have been doing for tens of thousands of years will become completely irrelevant!"

Acknowledgements

I wish to express my gratitude to the members of my writing group, who have vetted every chapter of this book, always with helpful suggestions for making it more interesting. This group is headed by Laurie Windham, and the other members are Jay Peck, Peg Thompson, Melissa Phillips, and Ilene Marcus.

The book was also given a professional editing by Catharine Bramkamp. I am always thankful for her efforts.

I also want to acknowledge the research work of Professors Dr. Jim B. Tucker and Dr. Bruce Grayson. Tucker's book *Return to Life*, Saint Martins Press, New York (2013) and Grayson's *After*, Saint Martins Publishing Group, New York (2021) planted the seeds of inspiration for this book. I thank them for their lifetimes of effort on furthering our understanding of the continuity of life experiences through death and of near-death experiences.

Finally, my wife Sidnee is an inspiration to everything I do. She provides a running commentary of suggestions during each project and supports my work with enthusiasm and humor. She also designed the cover for this book.

About the Author

Richard Boyd is an Emeritus Professor, having spent thirty years in the Physics and Astronomy Departments at The Ohio State University. He has worked extensively with collaborators in the United States and Japan, resulting in his authoring or coauthoring more than two-hundred-fifty articles on experimental and theoretical nuclear physics, astrophysics, and astrobiology. "When Computers Acquire Souls" is his tenth book. Two are scientific, one on nuclear astrophysics and the second on the origin of the molecules of life. The others are fictional. These include *Prairie Renaissance*; *Artificial Intelligence, Mankind at the Brink*; *Humans and Artificial Intelligence, Cooperation or Capitulation?* and *Irradiated, An Alien Perspective*. These are attempts to challenge some of the basic assumptions of twenty-first century humankind by wrapping them in interesting stories.

Made in the USA
Columbia, SC
23 May 2023

16656556R00085